bushfire

An Omnibus Book from Scholastic Australia

Teachers' notes for *Bushfire* are available from
www.scholastic.com.au

Omnibus Books
an imprint of Scholastic Australia Pty Ltd (ABN 11 000 614 577)
PO Box 579, Gosford NSW 2250.
www.scholastic.com.au

Part of the Scholastic Group
Sydney • Auckland • New York • Toronto • London • Mexico City
New Delhi • Hong Kong • Buenos Aires • Puerto Rico

First published in 2019.

A catalogue record for this book is available from the National Library of Australia

ISBN: 978-1-74299-430-7

Typeset in Minion 12pt/18pt.

Printed in China by Hang Tai Printing Company Limited.

26 27 28 / 2

bushfire

Sally Murphy

An Omnibus Book from Scholastic Australia

To the firefighters who fought in unfathomable conditions in February, 2009 – and to firefighters everywhere. Thank you. — SM

Chapter 1

'Mum, Gran's house is on TV!' I reach for the remote control on the coffee table and turn the sound up a little bit. Images of the terrible bushfire that hit Canberra five years ago flash across the screen. It is so eerie to see the orange glow over such a big city.

As Mum comes in from the kitchen, the scene changes from Gran's old street, blanketed under smoke, to firefighters trying to put out a burning house.

'Oh,' says Mum, drying her hands on a tea towel. 'That was such a terrible, terrible day.'

'I know. Gran must be very brave. Grandpa must have been too.' A tiny flicker of sadness goes through me when I say Grandpa's name. 'I think I would have just hidden under my bed.'

'Who's brave?' my brother Aaron asks, dragging his backpack into the lounge room. 'Me? For taking on Europe all alone?'

I laugh, but Mum's smile isn't as big.

'No, idiot,' I say. 'Gran. And the other people who were in Canberra when *that* happened.' I point at the

TV, not mentioning Grandpa again. 'Especially the firefighters. Now *they* must be super brave.'

Aaron ruffles my hair in his annoying big-brother way before plopping down next to me on the couch. 'Yeah, I guess,' he says. 'But why are they still talking about it?' He nods at the screen. 'Isn't it old news now?'

A commercial comes on and I turn the volume down a bit. 'It isn't just the Canberra fire,' I explain. 'It's about bushfires all over Australia, and how they were started. And how they put them out.' I pause for a moment. 'Like what Dad does. It's amazing, really. And dangerous.'

Dad works for Parks Victoria, looking after the forests around Healesville, where we live. In his spare time, he's a volunteer firefighter, so he gets called out to fight bushfires or to manage controlled burns, which are meant to help prevent the unpredictable, out-of-control fires.

'Yeah, I guess I never give it too much thought,' Aaron says. 'It's just something Dad's always done.'

'Maybe you *should* think more!' I say to Aaron.

He raises an eyebrow. 'Do I detect a lecture coming on?' he asks. 'You sound more and more like Mum every day. Save the planet. Save the trees, Save …'

I shrug, and give up. Usually if Aaron teases me I'd get more upset, but this is his last night at home and I don't feel like arguing. He's flying to London tomorrow, further away from us than he's ever been. Even Mum doesn't jump on what he's said—it's true, Mum does like to lecture us about taking care of the environment. But tonight she is unusually quiet.

I watch as Aaron drags his backpack towards him. Neither of the two zippers is closed, and stuff pokes out of both. His bag is bulging. His solution is to start pushing the clothes, trying to force them in, but as soon as he gets one thing in, something else pokes out.

Mum drops down on the chair across from him, pulling the bag towards her. 'Here, let me help,' she says. She unzips the bag and pulls everything out. Jeans, socks, undies, shirts, all cascade onto the floor in one big, tangled mess.

'Aaron!' Mum says, exasperated. 'Is this the washing I folded for you? Look what you've done.'

Aaron grimaces, looking a bit ashamed, and pulls the bag back towards him. 'Relax, Mum, I've got this.' He gives her a little smile. 'I've got to be able to look after myself, you know. You won't be there to repack my bag at the other end.'

Mum sighs. 'I know.' For a moment she looks really sad. 'But that's why I have to take this last opportunity to show you how to pack properly.'

It's Aaron's last day with us for a while. He can be a pain sometimes—like when he leaves his smelly clothes on the bathroom floor or drinks the last of the orange juice and puts the bottle back in the fridge empty—but he's also pretty good at playing games with me or helping with my homework, and last term he helped me make the most awesome Book Week costume ever. And, when Mum and Dad are busy at work, Aaron, being eight years older, looks after me or takes me places.

Except, he's leaving us. He's been saving since he was in Year Ten, with part-time work and holiday jobs, and now that he's finished school, he's off adventuring. Mum and Dad weren't so keen at first—they wanted him to wait till he'd finished university. But Aaron convinced them that, if he's old enough and organised enough to save for his trip, he's also sensible and organised enough to sort out a career when he gets home.

I watch the chaos of his backpack explode all over the room, with Mum tutting and sighing as she tries to sort it for him, and I wonder if he's really as organised as he claims.

As if he can read my thoughts, Aaron gives me a wink. 'It's nice of me to make Mum feel useful, isn't it?' His brown eyes twinkle.

Aaron and I laugh, but when a pair of socks hits him on the head, thrown by a cranky-looking Mum, he looks shame-faced for a second, till Mum cracks up laughing too.

'You dope,' she says. 'I'm going to miss you, Azza. But I will *not*'—she lobs another pair of socks his way—'miss doing your washing for you.'

'I'll miss you too, Mum.' Aaron winks at me again. 'And Amy has promised to start leaving dirty clothes around the place to make it feel like I'm still here.'

Mum laughs but not much, but I know that she must have a lump in her throat like I have in mine. When I look back at Aaron, who is now coiling his phone charger, I wonder if he has one too.

It's his first time away from home for anything more than a few nights—and he's heading to the other side of the world. I think he's pretty brave, going so far away.

The sound of wheels in the front driveway interrupts

my thoughts.

'Dad's home!' I say. I race to open the front door. He's really late home today.

His work clothes are filthy, his face is smudged with black stuff, and his hands, which he seems to have tried to wash, still have muddy streaks all over the backs of them.

'It's okay, Mum,' I call, smiling at Dad. 'Dad's gonna keep you in washing for a while.'

Dad looks confused, but when he puts his head into the lounge room to say hello, Aaron laughs with me, and even Mum smiles as they take in his appearance.

'Pah,' Mum says, shaking her head. 'He can wash his own.' She pats the pile of clothes she has just refolded, and hands them to Aaron.

Dad, still a bit confused, looks down at his work uniform. 'I guess it *is* a bit grubby,' he says. 'We had another controlled burn today. Imagine how dirty the full-time firies are!'

Mum frowns. 'I'll bet. But I'd also guess their firefighting gear doesn't go home to get washed.'

Dad shrugs. 'Maybe not. But do you want me to drive home naked?'

'Gross, Dad,' I say, trying not to imagine him driving naked. Mum lobs another pair of Aaron's socks at him.

Dad heads off to the laundry to take off his dirty clothes and Mum and Aaron turn back to the packing. I collect Aaron's socks from around the room. The lump is back in my throat and for once I don't feel like watching the rest of my TV show. Instead I press the off button and toss the remote onto the coffee table, heading for the kitchen.

'Amy, can you check the rice?' Mum calls after me. 'It's probably just about cooked.'

The kitchen is filled with the smell of one of Mum's delicious curries. On the stove the rice pot is bubbling and a stream of foamy gunk has run down the side of the pan. I quickly turn the heat down and grab a spoon to test the rice the way Mum has taught me.

'It's done!' I call through to the lounge room. 'Do you want me to drain it?'

'No, I'm here now.' Mum comes through the door, rubbing at her face. Has she been crying? She sees me looking and quickly smiles, but I know what she's thinking. She's going to miss Aaron as much as I will.

I give her a quick hug before I turn to start setting

the table. 'He'll be fine, Mum,' I say, repeating words she said to me a few days ago. 'It's only a year.'

Mum sighs. 'You're right. But we're going to miss him, aren't we?'

I nod, feeling tears tickling my own eyes. 'We are. But not his smelly clothes.'

Mum laughs, and by the time Dad and Aaron join us for dinner, we're both smiling again. This will be our last family dinner for a while, so we'd better enjoy it.

Later, as Dad clears the table and stacks the dishwasher, Aaron hands me a bowl of ice cream. 'Here,' he says. 'It's the last bit.'

I look at the delicious chocolate ice cream and then eye him suspiciously. Usually if the tub is nearly empty, we'd argue over it. 'You sure?' I ask. 'You didn't spit in it, did you?'

Aaron jabs me on the shoulder. 'Careful, Amy, or I might change my mind.'

I think for a moment, then grab a second bowl from the overhead cupboard, tipping half the ice cream in. 'There you go,' I say, handing it to him. 'Let's go halves.'

Aaron squints at his small serve of ice cream. 'Gee. Thanks. Your generosity knows no bounds.'

I look at my own tiny serve. Now that I've divided it we've only got a spoonful or so each. 'Hmm. Hardly worth it, is it? Do you want mine too?'

Dad turns from the dishwasher. 'Have I got this right? You guys are fighting over giving each other the last bit of ice cream?' He lunges towards us, one hand towards Aaron's bowl, the other towards mine. 'I can sort this one out,' he says. 'I'll have both!'

Aaron and I duck out of the way. 'No way, Dad!' I say.

As we eat our small serves of ice cream, Aaron and I smile at each other. 'You'll be able to eat *all* the ice cream while I'm gone,' says Aaron.

'Oi!' says Dad. 'What about me?'

Dad loves ice cream as much as Aaron and I do. I roll my eyes at Aaron. 'Not likely.'

Aaron grins.

That lump is back. 'I'm going to miss you, Azza.'

Aaron licks the last bit of ice cream from his spoon. 'Me too, Amester. But I'll write.'

'Letters?' I ask, wondering how long a letter would take from England, or Ireland, or any of the other places he's planning to visit.

‘Nah, you numpty. Emails. Might be a bit quicker. There’s internet cafes everywhere.’ He ruffles my hair. ‘Don’t worry, Amy. I’ll keep in touch. I’ll miss my little sis.’

It’s a perfect idea. I already have my own email account. When Gran stopped working as a teacher, she had a lot more time on her hands. She asked me to be her e-pal, as she called it, and fill her in on what was happening at my school—and everything else. Then she moved from Canberra to Marysville, so she could be closer to us, but we still email regularly. Marysville isn’t far away at all, a half-hour drive, but we don’t see her every day. But we’ll be seeing her tomorrow. She’s insisted on being there to wave Aaron off. She’s going to stop at the airport on her way back from visiting my Aunty Ev. At least seeing Gran will be a silver lining as Aaron flies off into the clouds.

Chapter 2

The next day starts with hustle and bustle, as Mum likes to call it.

'Mum, where's my clean undies?' Aaron calls. 'Dad, have you seen my phone charger?' I remember seeing him coiling it yesterday, but apparently he took it back out to charge his phone one more time.

Mum and Dad rush around trying to help Aaron with his last-minute lost items while I sit at the kitchen table, half-heartedly chewing my toast.

'Amy!' says Mum, rushing into the kitchen. 'Aren't you dressed yet? We're leaving for the airport in five minutes.'

Five minutes? Now I'm bustling too. I race to my bedroom and throw on my favourite jeans and the yellow T-shirt Aaron gave me for Christmas last year. I brush my hair, then grab my shoes from under my bed just as Mum calls again. 'Come *on*, Amy. We're leaving. Now.'

Still holding my shoes, I head for the front door, but in spite of Mum's worry, I'm the first one there. Dad is nowhere to be seen. Aaron is calling from the back door,

'I've just got to say goodbye to Buster.' I can't believe he's saying goodbye to his garden gnome! Mum is back in the kitchen.

As I stand waiting, she emerges with a container of cookies.

'Aaron's favourite,' she says when she sees me. 'Maybe he can take them on the plane.'

Poor Mum. I know she's feeling as bad as I do about Aaron leaving.

Dad must do too, because when he appears from the study, he has two sheets of information he's just printed out. 'Travel advisories,' he says, when Mum raises an eyebrow. 'From the government website.'

Finally we all make it to the car.

'Bye, house!' says Aaron as we reverse out the driveway. His smile is huge and excited, and he doesn't seem to notice that the rest of us are a bit quiet.

Mum's driving, and Dad reaches over and turns on the radio. News. *Boooring*. I start to ask Dad to change the station, but Mum shushes me.

'Leading climate change expert Professor Paul Sykes—' the announcer says, and I understand why Mum is so interested. I've never heard of Professor Sykes, but I know Mum will have. She works as a scientist at the university, where she's working on a research project looking at ways to stop or even reverse the effects of climate change. She's even won awards for her work on renewable energy.

As I slip my shoes on, Mum listens intently. After the interview, she smiles across at Dad. 'He's great,' she says. 'Really knows what he's talking about. He's got incredible ideas about the ways we can reduce emissions.'

As Mum and Dad chat away in the front, in the back seat, Aaron winks at me. 'Not going to miss long boring conversations about global warming, and ozone layers, and—'

'Oi!' Mum's says. 'I heard that!'

Aaron rolls his eyes. 'Here we go …' he mutters. He smiles as he says it though..

'It's your children who are going to suffer,' Mum says, looking back at Aaron in the rear-view mirror. 'When you have children, you'll know that you'll do anything and everything to protect them. You might even have to lecture them!'

'My children?' Aaron smirks. 'Who says I'm going to have children? I might enjoy travelling so much that I just spend the rest of my life roaming the world by myself.'

'Not likely!' Dad says. 'I've seen your bank balance. You'll have to come home eventually.'

We all laugh at that.

The drive to the airport is long. Soon we're leaving behind the green hills around our home and heading through endless suburbs. On the freeway we get stuck in heavy traffic for ages. 'Good thing we left early,' says Dad. His phone pings. 'It's Mum,' he says, turning round to talk to Aaron. 'She's already at the airport.'

'That's Gran,' says Aaron. 'Always early. I wonder if she baked me any goodies for the flight.'

Mum frowns. 'What about the cookies I made?'

'Oops.' Aaron holds up the now empty container. 'I thought they were for now.' He wipes biscuit crumbs off his lap, grinning. 'But they were yummy, by the way.'

Mum sighs dramatically, but she looks pretty pleased that Aaron liked her cookies. It's going to be a while before she can make him any more. 'You'll just have to eat airline food,' she says.

At the airport Gran is waiting near the check-in area. 'There you are!' she says, smiling when she sees us. 'I thought you'd never get here!'

'We said ten, Mum,' says Dad as he hugs her hello. 'And it's only just ten now.' Gran thinks if you're not at least ten minutes earlier than necessary then you're late.

Aaron gives Gran a quick hug before he takes his ticket over to check in. I hug her for a bit longer.

'Hi, Gran,' I say, holding her tight.

'How do you feel about your brother heading off?' Gran asks, when I let her go.

That's something I love about Gran. She always seems to ask the right question. 'Sad,' I say. 'But a bit excited for him too.'

Gran nods. 'Me too,' she says. 'And a teensy bit jealous,' she says. 'He's going places I've never been.'

I'm surprised by this. I mean, I know Gran has never travelled outside of Australia, but I'm surprised to hear her say she's jealous.

'But Gran,' I say, looking into her glittering deep blue eyes, 'you said you've never wanted to leave Australia.'

Gran shrugs. 'True,' she says. 'After all, there's so much to explore here in this wonderful country of ours that I could never hope to see it all, let alone the rest of the world.' She looks across at Aaron, who is jiggling on the spot while he waits in queue. 'But then I see how excited young Aaron is, and I think about London, and Paris—'

'And Venice!' I butt in. 'I wonder if he'll have a ride on one of those little boats.'

'Gondolas,' Gran says. 'And yes, Venice. I wonder, just a little bit, if I should have visited them while I was still young enough.'

I smile. Gran has never seemed old to me. She's active, and funny, and always learning and doing new things. 'You're still young enough,' I say. 'But don't go just yet,' I add, 'because then I'd have another person to miss.'

Gran frowns a little, thinking. 'You're right—I am young enough,' she says. 'Maybe it's not too late. But still, there are parts of Australia I could go and see too.'

Aaron returns, and then we make our way to the waiting area. Dad goes to get coffees and Aaron ducks into the gift shop. 'Just checking if they have any good munchies,' he says. 'For the flight.'

But when he returns, he has a flat-looking bag. He holds it out to me. 'No lollies,' he says, 'but I thought you might like this. An early Christmas present.'

'Thanks, Aaron.' Curious, I open the bag. Inside is a hardback book. The cover has a bright red background and is embossed with the words *Hard Times: Australia's*

Worst Natural Disasters. There are photos scattered across it—of flames and floods and broken-looking buildings.

'Do you like it?' Aaron is watching me closely.

'Like it?' I say. 'It's perfect!' I turn the book over and, on the back, find a list of what's included. 'It's got the Canberra fire, and Cyclone Tracy—'

Aaron holds up a hand. 'I know! I bought it, remember. And I know how you love to learn about every natural disaster that's ever happened. And then tell everyone about them. I'd call it a bit weird, but each to their own I suppose.' He winks.

'Who are you calling weird? But thanks, Aaron, it's brilliant.' I'm always watching shows about the power of nature, and survival, and cutting out stories from the newspaper and magazines for my pin-up board. Aaron reckons I'm a bit obsessed—and he might be right. Having a book like this with so many familiar stories—and some I haven't heard about before—is perfect. I'm really touched by his thoughtfulness.

I put the book down on the seat next to me and reach for a hug. 'Thank you!'

'You're welcome,' he says. 'I'm gonna miss you, little sis.' He squeezes harder before letting me go.

He looks at the departure board hanging nearby, flashing the names of cities around the world and flight numbers and times. 'I'd better go through to departures now,' he says. 'It's almost time.'

He jumps up and hugs Gran, then Dad and, last of all, Mum. As he turns to give me another hug, I see that his eyes are a bit shiny. His smile is still big, but it's kind of wobbly. I see Mum wipe a tear away, and Dad tries to smile, but doesn't quite manage it.

There are last-minute reminders and slaps on the back and more goodbyes, and then Aaron is gone through the gate, carrying his smaller backpack slung over his shoulder. I hope his big one, which he checked in, gets on the right plane. I've seen stories on airport shows on TV where people's luggage ends up in different countries or gets left behind. That wouldn't be fun.

We're all quiet in the car on the way home. Already we're missing Aaron. But I hold my book tight to my chest the whole way home. It's such a perfect present! I can't wait to start reading it.

Canberra Burns

Australia has a long history of bushfires, but few people expect such fires to enter our cities. That is exactly what happened in our capital city, Canberra, in January 2003, catching residents and authorities by surprise and causing widespread damage.

The fire, started by lightning in rural New South Wales several days earlier, had crept into the Australian Capital Territory. Efforts to control it were unsuccessful and, on 18 January, it spread into the suburbs of Canberra. Warnings to many residents came too late, and the fire spread quickly. Four hundred and seventy homes were damaged or destroyed, and four people were killed and almost 500 injured.

Most of the parks and bush around Canberra were burned, including the famous observatory at Mount Stromlo. Across Australia, people were astounded that such a thing could happen in our capital city. It was a reminder of the strength and unpredictability of fire and also highlighted changes that needed to be made in fire warning and management procedures.

Chapter 3

'Amy!' Trudi is waiting near the gate when I arrive at school on Monday. She has her schoolbag slung over one shoulder. She always waits for me before she goes in. 'How was your weekend?'

I pull a face. '*Okaaaay*,' I say. 'But Aaron left.' I can't believe how much I miss him and it's only been two days.

Trudi gives me a sympathetic look as we walk towards our classroom. 'Oh, I forgot. Did you go to the airport?'

'Yep.' I hang my bag on the hook next to hers. 'That was pretty cool. And he bought me a present.' I tell her all about my new book.

'Sounds more interesting than my weekend, anyway,' says Trudi.

I feel bad that I haven't thought to ask her. I've been so caught up in my own stuff. 'What did you do?' I ask her.

'Nothing,' Trudi sighs. 'A big fat nothing. Unless you count helping Mum in the garden.'

I've always liked the garden at Trudi's house. 'Well,

that's something, isn't it?' I ask.

'I guess,' says Trudi. 'Mum had me carting washing machine water to water everything.' She sighs. 'Smelly water. One bucket at a time. It took *aaages*.'

I frown. 'Why washing machine water?' I ask.

Trudi rolls her eyes. 'The water restrictions,' she sighs. 'Stuff's starting to die because Mum can't use the retic. So now she has us reusing every drop we can. She even wants us to stand in a basin in the shower so she can use our dirty shower water instead of letting it go down the drain!'

'Gross,' I say. But then I think of all the flowers and trees in Trudi's garden. 'But I guess if it keeps everything alive it might be worth it?'

'I guess so. As long as she doesn't use shower water in the veggie patch!' She looks horrified at the thought.

I pause, thinking about this. I'm not sure I understand how shower water on the vegie patch is different from shower water on the rest of the garden.

'You know, I could be eating tomatoes fed by water I've showered in. Or Mum,' Trudi explains.

'Eeeeww.' I screw up my nose. 'I hadn't thought of that!'

In class, we sit together. Ms Yeap lets us, though she sometimes says we distract each other. Trudi and I like Ms Yeap, even when she makes us work hard. Mostly she makes learning fun, with lots of group work and interesting projects.

'Take out your maths books,' Ms Yeap says, after the usual good morning and roll checking.

There are a few groans, including from me. I much prefer when we start with reading or writing. But my mind doesn't stay on maths for long—because there is a surprise waiting for me when I open my desk.

A spider has chosen *my* desk—of all the desks in the classroom—to hide in, creepily crawling across my maths book as I open the tray and pull it out.

I jump up out of my chair, flinging the book away, and scream. Very loudly.

The whole class stops what they are doing. A few other people gasp when they see the big hairy spider, but no one else reacts as dramatically as I do.

'Look at Amy!' Leith, the boy who sits across from me, says. 'She's gonna cry!'

'Back off, Leith.' Trudi seems to always come to my rescue. Not only does she tell Leith off, but then she uses her ruler to scoop the spider onto her own maths book and carries it carefully to the classroom door. 'Can I go put it in the garden?' she asks Ms Yeap.

Ms Yeap, who looks a tiny bit scared herself, nods. 'I think that might be best,' she says.

By the time Trudi comes back, the classroom is back to normal. Most people are back at work, puzzling their way through their maths exercises, but my cheeks are bright red with embarrassment. And I'm still shaking. Spiders are just one of the many things I'm scared of.

I give Trudi a grateful look and mouth 'thank you'. She grins and gives me a thumbs up before opening her maths book.

I open mine too and pretend to work, but my hand is still shaking.

What makes it worse is that Leith seems to think what just happened is hilarious.

I hear him singing 'Incy Wincy Spider' quietly so that Ms Yeap can't hear and, when I glance over at him, he links his hands to imitate a huge spider crawling across the desk towards me.

I try to ignore him, but I know he can tell I'm still embarrassed.

I look down at my desk, wishing he would leave me alone.

After maths, Ms Yeap writes the word 'persuasion' on the board. It's a word we've used a lot this term. We've been learning about persuasive writing and started by practising persuasive speaking. That was fun. We learnt that just saying *pleeeeaaaasee* slowly and hopefully, like we do at home when we want something, isn't as effective as having some good arguments prepared. Using these newfound techniques, I even managed to get a pocket money raise from my parents when I was able to argue that it would teach me budgeting and fiscal responsibility. Mum was impressed by the big words!

'Now,' says Ms Yeap, 'we're going to start putting all those persuasive techniques into a longer piece of writing.'

There are a few groans around the room, though not as many as there were at the start of maths. Not everybody loves writing, even though I do, and some people, like Shelby Knowles, groan about *everything*.

'And,' Ms Yeap continues, pretending she hasn't heard the grumbles, 'since this is our last big piece of writing for the year'—she pauses as some people cheer—

'it's your chance to demonstrate not just your persuasive techniques but also all you've learnt about writing throughout the year.' She beams at us all as if she has just delivered the most exciting piece of news ever.

The task she sets sounds difficult. We have to research and write an essay convincing readers to take some sort of action about an issue we care about.

'Like recess?' asks Shelby. Recess is the only thing Shelby doesn't complain about. And lunchtime.

Ms Yeap frowns. 'Not quite, Shelby.' She thinks for a moment. 'I'm hoping you care about something more than recess. You can't simply convince me to let you have more recess, since I am not your audience. I want you to imagine that you are convincing somebody important to make a change.'

'Like Mrs Armstrong?' Shelby asks, naming our school principal.

Ms Yeap considers this. 'I guess so. But there has to be some evidence to support what you argue. So if you *must* use recess as your topic, Shelby'—she looks unconvinced still—'then you must show why longer recess, or an extra recess break, or whatever it is you want, is important.' She looks around the room. 'Can anyone think why extra recess could be beneficial?'

Lots of hands go up. 'It's fun!' says Shelby.

'Less maths,' says Jonah. Even I can see the good side of that.

'More time for snacks!' says Mo. We all giggle.

'*Yeees*,' says Ms Yeap. 'But do you think any of these things would convince Mrs Armstrong, or even the Minister for Education, to give you more recess time?'

More groans. She's right. Adults don't seem to think fun, and even snacks, are important.

But then Mo surprises us all by putting his hand up again. 'So, you're saying it needs to be not just about us?'

Ms Yeap smiles and nods.

'So, what about that we get more time outside, which means more Vitamin—' He pauses. 'You know, the vitamin we get from the sun.'

Ms Yeap claps her hands together enthusiastically. 'Vitamin D! Excellent point, Mo.' Mo smiles proudly. 'And yes, that's what I mean.' She looks at Shelby. 'So if you choose recess, you could research the benefits of Vitamin D as a starting point.'

Shelby looks relieved and even smiles at Mo gratefully.

We start by talking about our ideas with our partners. I turn to Trudi, trying to ignore Leith, who might be talking to the boy next to him, Brendan, but is still making his hands into a giant spider on the desk.

'I want to do natural disasters,' I say, still thinking about my new book. 'Maybe I could do Stuart Diver.'

'Not again!' Trudi interrupts. 'You did him for the biography project last term. Come on, Amy, this is getting ridiculous.'

She's probably right. Stuart Diver was the only survivor of a landslide in the Snowy Mountains, on the same day I was born. I think that's what really stuck with me, that we somehow shared that day. Mum had told me about him on my eighth birthday. We had gone up to Lake Mountain, just up from Marysville, where Aaron and I go tobogganing almost every winter. I couldn't imagine what it would have felt like to be in a wintery wonderland that suddenly became deadly. I've been completely fascinated by natural disasters ever since.

I reach for a piece of paper and start listing all the interesting events from my book: cyclones, bushfires, earthquakes, floods.

Ms Yeap, who is patrolling the room, stops to read

what I've written. 'Disasters again, Amy?' she asks, sighing a little.

I nod enthusiastically.

'It would be nice to see you extend yourself a bit,' Ms Yeap says. 'And remember you need to persuade us about something. And not just that they are interesting.' How did she know that's what I was thinking? 'You're trying to get your reader keen to make a change.'

I pause, my pen in my mouth. I wonder if there's a way to convince people to avoid natural disasters? But of course most people don't choose to get caught up in them, except storm chasers.

Ms Yeap continues. 'Of course, you *could* do a different topic for a change.' I try not to roll my eyes while I wait for her to explain what she means. 'Isn't there anything else you care about? Anything earth-shattering?'

Like ridding the world of spiders? I think this, but don't say it out loud. I don't want to give Leith any more ammunition.

As Ms Yeap wanders off to check on other students, an idea jumps into my head. 'Climate change!' I say to Trudi. 'Mum was saying that some of our natural disasters are the result of climate change.'

'I bet,' Trudi says. Even Trudi has heard Mum's talks about global warming and how we need to take action. 'All *my* mum talks about is water restrictions.'

I look at her, one eyebrow raised, waiting for her to make the connection. It only takes a moment.

'That's *my* topic!' Trudi says, excited. 'Drought, and water restrictions, and what we can do to save water. Mum will have lots of ideas for me.'

'And my mum will have lots for me,' I say as we high-five each other. 'Sorted!'

Chapter 4

I can't wait for Mum to get home from work. I flop in front of the TV, but I listen out for the sound of her car in the driveway.

'Mum!' I say, as soon as she comes through the door. 'I have to write an essay for school, and guess what topic I'm doing?'

'Hello to you too, Amy,' she says. She pretends to think about my question, scratching her head. 'Ummmmm—Stuart Diver?'

I shake my head. For once I'm not being predictable. 'Guess again.' I don't tell her he was my first choice.

'The cyclone that hit Darwin?'

'Cyclone Tracy. But nope.'

Mum shrugs. I have her stumped. 'That flood in 19—'

'Nopity nope.' I cut her off. 'You'll never guess!' I say.

Mum laughs, her green eyes sparkling. 'Then why ask me to guess?'

She has a point there. 'Climate change!' I say.

Mum smiles. 'Now *that* sounds cool,' she says.

'Could it be that my message is getting through to you after all?' She puts her bag down on the hall table and heads towards the kitchen. I follow.

'Yep,' I say, grabbing an apple from the fruit bowl. 'Plus, you'll be able to help me.'

'Aaah. Now the truth comes out. You just happened to choose a topic that your mum knows lots about so you could get some free help.'

'You will, won't you?' I try my cute face, eyes opened wide, lips in a little tight smile. '*Pleeease?*'

Mum raises an eyebrow. Then I remember what Ms Yeap has taught us about persuasive techniques.

'See, I know it's such an important area for people to hear about,' I begin. 'But I need to support what I'm saying with evidence, so people will take me seriously.' I try to keep my face serious as I look Mum in the eye. 'And who better to help with that evidence than a scientist like you?' I take a bite of the apple.

Mum throws her hands in the air. 'Flattery will get you everywhere! It really is an important topic. Maybe we can start tonight after dinner?' she suggests.

'Thanks, Mum,' I say, giving her a hug. 'Would you like some help with dinner?' I add. If I want her to help me, I'd better be sure to help her too. Besides, I love cooking with Mum.

Later, after dinner is eaten and I've helped Dad with the dishes, Mum brings her laptop to the kitchen table, where I've spread out my homework.

'So, what is it you want to know?' she asks.

I look at my page, blank except for the words *Climate Change* and *Global Warming*. 'Umm. Everything!' I say.

'Everything? I have an office full of books and papers, and there are hundreds of research papers written on this topic every year. Are you sure you want to know everything?' She looks at my piece of paper. 'Or that you can fit it all into this one essay?'

She's right. As always. Mum's been studying and writing about climate change for years. I only have a couple of weeks to finish my essay. I think for a moment. 'So maybe I could start with explaining what climate change and global warming are, then why it's important we try to stop them from happening?'

Mum nods. 'Sure. And then perhaps what can be done on a local level.'

I stop writing, frowning.

Mum sees that I'm not following her. 'You know,

what ordinary people like you or your friends can do about it?'

I sigh. I'm not sure there's anything a kid like me can do. Climate change is huge—a global issue. And I'm just a school kid who's scared of spiders.

Mum types an address into her web browser, turning the screen towards me. 'Look,' she says, pointing at the title of the article she's brought up. 'Five things you can do about climate change.'

The list doesn't seem very complicated. It includes things like walking places whenever you can instead of driving, reducing waste and recycling.

'These don't seem like big things,' I say to Mum. 'Can recycling my drink bottles really stop global warming?'

'Definitely!' I love the way Mum's voice gets somehow brighter when she talks about things she's passionate about. 'See, one drink bottle might not seem to make a difference. But it's the plastics that are used to make new bottles, and the transport costs, and the water, and everything that goes into making each bottle that's the problem.' She pauses for a breath. 'So if *you* start recycling them—or, better still, avoid using the plastic bottles in the first place—and then someone else does, and someone else does, then change starts to happen. That's why I only drive to the train station rather than all the way to the university.'

I'm starting to see her point. 'So, it's lots of people making little changes that start to make a big change?' I ask.

'Exactly!' Mum says. 'You're a smart cookie, Amy.'

Dad chooses just that moment to come in from the study. 'Did someone mention cookies?' he asks. 'I'm starving.'

Mum and I giggle. As I make notes on the things Mum and I have talked about, I feel a tingle of excitement. This is a good topic. And an important one. It even links to natural disasters. I can't wait to start writing about it.

But first, Dad makes hot chocolate and brings out a container of cookies. Maybe there's time for dessert before I do any more work.

While we sit and drink our hot chocolate, Mum's phone pings. She smiles when she picks it up. 'At last!' she says. 'It's from Aaron.' She reads out his message.

Hi Mum. Got to London okay. Planes are fun, but glad to be here at last. London is big. And noisy. And just like on TV. Got to sleep now. Jet lagged. Hugs to Amy and hello to Dad xx

I'm glad we've heard from Aaron, but his text reminds me how much I miss him. Some of the glow of excitement about the assignment wears off. I can feel myself frown.

'It's okay, Amy,' Dad says. 'He'll be home before you know it.'

I hope so. But I know I should be happy that he's off having an adventure.

Chapter 5

Dear Amy

Wow. London is really busy. I've ridden on lots of those double-decker buses like you see on TV, and on the underground, which is a train system that goes everywhere. I don't like the trains as much as the buses, cos you can't see anything under the ground. Just tunnel walls, and all the other people hurrying to get places. It seems like everyone here is in a hurry.

The plane trip was long and boring. We stopped in Dubai, but I only got to see the airport. What a big airport but! Filled with shops and cafés and people. So many people. And there's a whole hotel in the airport.

I'm writing this on the computer in the lounge of the hostel. The hostel is old but it's cheap. There are lots of other travellers from all over the world, and I've met some guys from New Zealand. They've heard about some farm work going, and I'm going to see if I can get a job with them too. It's near a place called Devon.

You can share this email with Mum and Dad if you like, and tell them I'll write to them soon too. Give them my love.

Aaron

When Mum gets home I tell her about Aaron's email. She comes and reads it over my shoulder.

'Farm work?' she says. 'Well, it's a job, and a good way to see the place. It's a bit different from his last job.'

I laugh. Aaron spent every weekend for the last six months working at a play centre—one of those places where kids have birthday parties and then race all over the indoor play equipment. Whenever there was a party, Aaron had to dress up as a clown and organise the games and stuff. He didn't like it that much, but he always said 'It's worth it if it gets me to Europe!' when he got home.

Mum seems a bit distracted. 'Actually,' she says, as she perches on the arm of the couch, looking serious. 'How would you feel if *I* went to work in Europe too, just for a little while?'

I've got no idea what Mum's talking about, but with Aaron, then Gran, now Mum, it suddenly seems like everyone is planning trips. 'Why?' I ask. 'When?'

'Don't look so worried,' Mum says. 'It's not definite yet. But there are these people in Brussels who have been doing some really interesting research a bit like mine. And they're having a symposium.'

'A what?' I ask. I try to sound calm, but inside my

tummy is fluttering unpleasantly. With Aaron already gone, I really don't want Mum to go away too.

'A big meet-up of experts, to share knowledge and ideas talking about renewable energy sources.' She reaches over to her briefcase, which is sitting on the coffee table. 'The Dean gave me this brochure today. The university is very keen for me to go. There's funding available for me to attend.'

I glance at the brochure, but don't give it too much attention. Instead I try to look interested while Mum talks about the possible trip and how much she would learn and what a wonderful opportunity it would be. Finally, though, she must notice that I'm not saying much. 'What's the matter?' she asks.

I shake my head. I don't want to speak because I know I'm being a bit selfish not wanting her to go.

Mum hugs me. 'Oh, I'm sorry,' she says, even though I still haven't said anything. 'I guess it's not very exciting for you to think about me going away for a while. Especially while Aaron's away too.' She looks down at the brochures. 'But it wouldn't be for too long, and maybe Dad could take some time off work, and …'

'It's fine, Mum,' I say, finally finding my voice. This

is a moment where I can try to be brave. 'It sounds interesting. And important.' I point to my homework folder, where all my notes on climate change are. 'We need people like you working on a solution. You should totally go. Dad and I will be fine.'

Mum frowns. 'But it's in January. During the school holidays. And that's when I usually take time off so we can do stuff together. It wouldn't be fair for me to go off on my own.'

I think about this. 'How long would you go for?' I ask.

'Two weeks. A bit longer if I also wanted to spend time with Aaron.'

Two weeks is a long time. I've never been more that two days without seeing Mum. My heart is a heavy ball in my chest, but I think of all I've been reading about global warming, and about how much Mum must miss Aaron. Suddenly an idea pops into my head.

'Gran!' I say. 'I can go and stay with Gran for a while. That would be so fun!' Gran has been promising a sleepover with just me and her ever since she moved to Marysville, but it hasn't happened so far. School holidays would be a perfect time. I feel excited at the thought of having Gran to myself for a while.

Mum smiles. 'Now that could work,' she says, thinking. 'Of course, we'd have to ask her.'

'She'll say yes,' I say, feeling better about the idea now that I've thought of a plan of my own. 'You should totally do it, Mum!'

Mum smiles. 'We'll see,' she says, but she looks longingly at the brochure in her hands. 'It's not definite, and I haven't even had a chance to talk to Dad about it yet.'

But as she gets up off the couch, I know that she really wants to go.

'Is Brussels anywhere near where Aaron is?' I ask.

Mum smiles. 'Everything is close in Europe, compared to Australia!' she says. 'I think I'd be able to catch up with him somehow, even if it means a bit of a detour.' Her eyes shine.

'That seals it, then,' I say, suddenly feeling a bit happier. 'You should definitely go and check up on that brother of mine. I know how much you miss him.'

Mum nods. 'I do miss him,' she says. 'And you're right, it's a great chance to see him, in between the work. But don't mention it to him in your emails just yet. Just in case it doesn't go ahead. Now,' she says, changing the subject, 'don't you have some homework to do? I bet you haven't finished that essay yet.'

She's right, though I have nearly finished my first draft. I go and get my school bag and pull out my workbooks. I'd really rather be watching TV or replying to Aaron's email, or reading *Hard Times: Australia's Worst Natural Disasters*, but I guess I'd better do some work first.

As I read through my draft, I shiver a little, and realise there is one thing I haven't explained and I don't really understand. 'Mum,' I ask. She looks up from the book she's reading. 'If global warming is making everything heat up, how come it's so cold today? It's almost summer. And there was snow on Mount Kosciuszko the other week!' I add, remembering seeing a news report about it.

Mum nods. 'Yes, that was unusual. And on cooler days like today I seem to always be answering people's questions checking if global warming is real. It's complicated to explain, but I guess that's why the term "climate change" helps. I suppose that the simplest way to explain it is that it means more extreme weather, more often.'

I put my pen down and lean forward. Mum has the

intense look on her face she gets when she talks about her special subject and, after the research I've been doing, I'm much more interested than I used to be.

'You see, we know that the global temperature is rising, but weather is measured daily, whereas climate is measured on long-term trends. So global warming doesn't mean it will be stinking hot every day'—she leans towards me—'but on average our temperatures are higher than they were—and are continuing to rise.'

I nod. I think I understand.

'And as changes happen, weather events change too—so big storms and extremes are seen in places they haven't been seen before.'

'So climate change causes storms?'

Mum shrugs. 'We can't point at any one storm and say that it was caused by climate change—because storms have always happened.' She pauses to see if I understand. 'But we can study the regularity and location of storms, looking for new patterns. Even with snowfall,' she says, obviously thinking about what I said about Kosciuszko.

'See, to make snow, the atmosphere needs moisture. And where does that moisture come from?'

'Evaporation?' I ask, pretty sure I know the answer.

'Exactly!' Mum raises a finger in the air, looking pleased that I knew the answer. 'Higher temperatures mean more evaporation.'

I usually love snow. Snow means trips to Lake Mountain, and snow fights and tobogganing. But snow at the wrong time of the year can cause problems. And if it's a sign of climate change, then that's a big problem!

'Hey, Mum!' I say, as the reality of what she is telling me starts sinking in, 'you *have* to go to Europe!'

Mum doesn't say much, but she smiles and nods, and I know that she will go.

I turn back to my essay. I have to convince people to do everything they can to stop harming the environment.

A week later I'm not so pleased that I worked so hard on my essay.

'Your essay was wonderful!' Ms Yeap tells me.

I smile proudly.

'So good that I've chosen it to be read out at assembly next week.'

I feel the smile drop off my face. I'm surprised I don't hear it thud on the floor. The end-of-year assembly! She wants me to stand up in front of everyone and read out my essay?

'I …' I begin, not sure what to say. Panic floods through my veins.

Ms Yeap sees my face and smiles reassuringly. 'You'll be fine,' she says, patting my arm. 'Brilliant, in fact. Your essay is important and deserves to be shared.'

I swallow. Well, I do want to raise awareness about what kids like me and my schoolmates can do to stop global warming. The thought of standing up in front of everyone fills me with terror, but so does the thought of what will happen to the earth if we don't act soon.

Chapter 6

'Still raining!' I say, looking miserably out the back window. 'Trudi and I wanted to go swimming today!'

Dad smiles. 'Well, there's plenty of water for it. You won't even need to go to the pool!'

I try to smile, but I'm annoyed. The school holidays are finally here and they're being ruined by the rain. Outside, a towel that was left on the clothesline flaps soggily in the wind. Across the yard there are muddy puddles everywhere, and the drain pipe on the wall of the back shed is gushing water onto the ground. I don't think I've ever seen so much rain. I wonder if it's been enough now to declare the drought over.

It's still raining when Dad drops me off at Trudi's house on his way to work half an hour later. He's whistling. I think he likes working more when it's like this. No fires to control.

Trudi's house is right near the Healesville Sanctuary, a zoo that takes care of protected native species. I think it's cool that Trudi has amazing birds and wallabies and dingoes as neighbours. Trudi always jokes that this is why her mum is so into her garden. Her mum looks after the flora while their neighbours look after the fauna.

Trudi opens the door. 'No school!'

'Yeah,' I say, not feeling half as cheerful as she seems to be as I follow her down the hallway to the kitchen. 'But it's supposed to be summer. Look at all this rain!' I point out of the kitchen window to the backyard.

Trudi's mum hears me. 'Yes, just look at it!' She beams. 'Isn't it wonderful?' she says, pointing at her garden. 'I can almost hear my plants gulping down all that precious water.'

I hadn't thought of that. I've been so busy thinking about my plans being spoilt that I forgot about the good side of the rain. I think back to Trudi's essay about the effects of drought. 'I guess that's a really good thing, isn't it?' I say, feeling a bit happier. 'Not just your garden, but everyone else's—'

'And the dams!' says Trudi. 'Maybe if there's enough rain then the water restrictions will stop.'

'I think we would need a lot more rain for that to happen,' Trudi's mum says. 'But yes, maybe the drought is breaking. That would be wonderful!'

I realise I've been a bit selfish complaining about the

rain. 'Still,' I say, 'it would be nice if it could just rain at night, so that we could still go to the pool in the daytime!'

Trudi nods. 'Yeah. So what shall we do instead?'

'I dunno. What were you doing before I got here?'

'Playing on the computer,' says Trudi. 'I was mucking around with a photo program. Come and have a look.'

Trudi is lucky enough to have a computer in her bedroom. We head to her room, and she shows me what she's been doing.

'It's me. On the moon!' she says, pointing at the screen.

Sure enough, the photo on her monitor shows a dusty grey surface like I've seen on documentaries about the moon and there's an astronaut in a full space suit. But the face in the visor is Trudi's.

'How did you do that?' I ask.

'Easy!' says Trudi. 'I've also done me scuba diving, and Mum on top of the Sydney Opera House.' She clicks through to the other images she has saved.

'Cool.' I say. 'Can I do one?'

We spend the rest of the morning cutting and pasting and making photos of ourselves doing all sorts of things. We even manage to make ourselves into mermaids.

'Let's print this one out,' says Trudi. I smile again at the sight of Trudi with flowing orange locks and a hot pink tail, and me with a purple one and bright green hair. It's silly, but fun.

When it's printed, I have a great idea.

'I reckon this would be a cool present for someone,' I say. 'Maybe for Christmas.'

Just then Trudi's mum calls from down the hallway. 'Girls. Don't you think you've been on the computer long enough?'

Trudi sighs. But when we look at the clock we realise it's been two hours! 'What else do you want to do?' asks Trudi, standing up reluctantly.

I stand too, stretching. We really have been sitting down for a long time.

Trudi's mum appears in the doorway. 'It's stopped raining,' she says. 'You should get outside for a while.'

In the backyard, everything is wet. 'Petrichor! Smell that!' says Trudi, taking a deep breath.

'Petri-what?' I ask.

'It's that smell after the rain. It's got a name.'

I take a deep breath in. There is a smell of wet earth, and damp trees, and cool. It smells nice.

'It seems greener than it was just a few days ago,' says Trudi. 'Some of those vegetable plants were almost dead, and now look at them.' She points at the vegie patch, where green tomato plants and lettuces are growing.

'Looks like you'll have lots of veggies!' I say.

'I guess that's a good thing,' she says.

Trudi's mum has come outside too and is smiling as she moves around the garden, checking on her precious plants. 'I don't believe it!' she says, stooping down. 'A weed already!' She holds up the tiny offending piece of green, which I can only just see, it is so tiny. 'A little bit of rain and everything flourishes.'

'Great,' says Trudi. 'You'll have me out here weeding all holidays if this keeps up.'

Her mum laughs. 'Oh, I hope so!'

I don't want the rain to keep up—or to help with weeding—but I guess if that means the end of the drought it wouldn't be the worst thing ever.

Dear Aaron

You won't believe it but it's still raining. Feels like it hasn't stopped all week. It's supposed to be summer, and the weather bureau says we could be heading for our wettest December on record. It's good news, I suppose, with the drought having gone on for so long. I hope it doesn't rain on Christmas.

It's going to be funny not having you here for Christmas. It's going to be just me, Mum and Dad, and Gran. She's going to come over for the day before heading to Aunt Ev's for Boxing Day. We'll miss not having you here, but I wonder if you'll miss us too or if you're too busy having fun. Will you still be working in Devon at Christmas or will you have gone somewhere else? And does it snow in Devon? I wonder if you'll have a white Christmas.

Mum is very excited about seeing you in January. I think she might even be more excited about seeing you than she is about her research trip, if that's possible. I'm trying not to be jealous that she'll get to see you, and that both of you will be in Europe while I stay home with just Dad.

You guys will have snow and each other and Europe, and I'll be home, on the school holidays, all by my lonesome self.

Write soon and cheer me up. I'm attaching a photo of Buster. Mum let me borrow her camera. As you can see, he doesn't like the rain either.

Amy

Chapter 7

I can't wait to see Gran at Christmas. I've been working on a special Christmas present for her. Editing photos with Trudi gave me the idea. I've found photos of famous holiday destinations online to make Gran a special photo book.

Mum comes to look at what I'm doing on the computer. 'The Eiffel Tower?' she says. 'I want to go there when I'm in Paris!' Then she looks a bit closer. 'Is that Gran?' She smiles as she realises that I've edited the photo so Gran is in front of the tower. 'Oh, did you do that?'

'Yep. She's also going to the Great Wall of China, and to see Big Ben and even to Antarctica.' I click through and show Mum the photos. 'I'm going to print them out and make a present for Gran for Christmas.'

Mum laughs. 'Oh, that's funny! I think she'll really like that. But what inspired this?'

I tell her about Gran and I talking about travel when Aaron was leaving.

'Oh. Funny, she's never really talked about going overseas before,' Mum says. 'But she should totally go, while she's still able. Though'—she looks again at the last photo, the one in Antarctica – 'I'm not sure she should be heading to Antarctica. Polar trekking might be a bit much for her.'

I giggle. Mum's probably right, but it's a fun photo—one of my favourites. I can't wait to give it to Gran. I've made a little one for Aaron too. I used the photo I took of Buster the gnome and edited it so that he's peeking out behind Aaron in one of the photos he sent of himself in front of Big Ben. I'll email it to him for Christmas.

Later Mum and I head out to the shops. The shopping centre is packed with people. Everyone seems to be in a hurry, carrying bags and parcels and racing from shop to shop and in and out of the carpark. Christmas carols are playing, but lots of people look stressed.

I'm not sure why people get so busy and worried at Christmas. 'Aren't they supposed to be happy?' I ask Mum. 'Christmas is the best time of the year!'

Mum looks around at all the grumpy-looking people. 'You're right,' she says. 'But I guess it's easy to forget to be happy when you're busy trying to get everything done. All the shopping and cooking, and making sure everyone gets a present …'

'So they make themselves unhappy trying to make sure everyone else is happy?' I ask.

'When you put it like that, it does sound silly,' she says.

Just then a new song comes over the shopping centre loudspeaker. 'Joy to the world' starts blaring through the speakers.

'See,' I say, 'the music is reminding them they're supposed to feel joy! They need a song to tell them how to act!'

Mum laughs, and I giggle. I see a lady look at us and, for a moment, she smiles too. Maybe we are spreading some joy.

'Merry Christmas, Gran,' I say, passing her the carefully wrapped present and giving her a hug. 'Open it!' I can't wait for her to see the photobook that I made for her.

I watch her carefully unstick the tape from the end of the package. Across the room, Mum and Dad are busy unwrapping their presents. Mum is careful like Gran but Dad just rips the paper off his, like I have been doing with mine.

'Gran's World Tour.' Gran reads the cover of the book, frowning slightly. 'What's this?'

I watch as she turns the pages looking at first confused and then amused. A big smile lights up her face. 'Oh!' she says, peering closely at the scene of her standing in front of the Leaning Tower of Pisa. 'It's me!' She flips back a page. 'Oh, that's me too,' she says, looking more closely at the photo of Niagara Falls, where I've added her looking over the falls.

'You're in all of them!' I tell her, pointing over her shoulder.

'Did you do this, Amy?' she asks. When I nod, she adds, 'You're so clever. It must have taken ages.'

It did, but I don't tell her that. Instead I shrug. 'Nah. It was easy. And fun.'

She smiles. 'Well, I won't need to book that trip now, will I?'

I frown, not understanding. Why wouldn't she want to visit those amazing places?

She giggles, tapping the book. 'Now that I've already been everywhere, I can just sit back and relax.'

I laugh too, getting her joke. 'It's supposed to make

you keener to go! I bet the real photos will be even better.'

'You might be right,' Gran says as she continues to turn pages. 'But I'm not sure I'll be going to all these places. Is that Antarctica?' she asks, stopping at the page that Mum liked. 'Too cold for me! But this so funny!'

She puts the book down and gives me a hug. 'Best present ever.'

Dad looks up from where he is busy emptying his Christmas stocking. 'Oi!' he says. 'What about all the presents I've given you over the years?'

'Okay,' says Gran, pretending to look shame-faced. 'The equal best. With all the macaroni necklaces your dad made me when he was at school.' She gives me a wink.

Christmas morning is fun, and I love having Gran there, but I can't help missing Aaron. We're going to phone him later, but the time difference means that he'll still be asleep over in England at the moment. Strange to think that it isn't really Christmas yet where he is.

Mum unwraps her present from Gran. 'Gloves!' she says. 'How thoughtful.' She puts on the woolly purple gloves and shows them off.

I'm a bit confused. Why would Mum need woolly gloves in summer? But then I remember that in just a few weeks she'll be flying to Europe, where it's winter. I try not to feel sad at the thought. It's Christmas and I should be happy.

My own present from Gran is sitting on the coffee table. I've been too busy watching Gran enjoy her photo book.

'Aren't you going to open it?' Gran asks, seeing me looking.

'Of course,' I say, ripping the paper off enthusiastically. Gran always gives great presents.

'Oh, wow!' I say, squealing excitedly. 'A digital camera!'

I drop the box onto the couch and give Gran a big hug. 'Thank you so much! I've wanted a proper camera for ages!'

'I know!' says Gran, releasing me. 'And I can't wait to see what you do with it. You can add photos to your emails to me.'

'And to Aaron!' I say. 'We can send him one of us all today!'

First, though, I have to work out how to use the camera. I carefully open it and start reading the instructions. There are lots of buttons and things to get used to, but I can't wait to be able to snap some shots to send Aaron.

'If it's easy to use, maybe you can teach me,' says Gran. 'Then I'll be able to get one for when I go travelling.'

'It's a deal,' I say. 'And maybe I can edit myself into the photos you take!'

Dear Amy

Merry Christmas! I know I said it once already, but I'm saying it again in writing now that I'm properly awake. It was great to wake up to a phone call from you all—but it did mean I might not have sounded very sensible. Me and the boys had a late night last night.

Today we have had a fairly quiet Christmas. Very different from home. The boss's wife made us all come and have lunch with them—four backpackers, her and the boss, Robert, and his elderly parents. It was nice of them to have us, but it was very formal—a full roast turkey with all the trimmings. But no Christmas crackers or silly jokes or anything.

I was a bit disappointed to discover that, even in England, white Christmases are rare. It would have been pretty cool to wake up to snow, and maybe even have a snow fight or build a snowman. But it wasn't to be. Instead it was very, very cold and fine. Even a bit of blue sky. Still, I bet there will be plenty of snow in January and February, and I'll be complaining about the cold.

Thanks for the cool photo of me and Buster. Maybe I should have brought him with me—would have made for some great photo opportunities. Thanks too for the one of Mum, Dad and Gran. Shame you couldn't be in the picture too. Does your camera have a timer? I wonder if anyone will ever come up with a better way of taking photos of yourself. Still, you could have got one of them to take a photo of you! Do that next time—I have to keep an eye on my little sis.

The work on the farm has been quite interesting. They have a big shed of turkeys, which meant the lead-up to Christmas was super busy. I've learnt to drive a tractor, and take hay to the cows. The other guys have been helping with some repairs. There was a massive storm in the area back in October, with flooding and big hail. Bad for the farm, good for us because they would normally only hire one worker, but decided they would get a group of us for a month to get everything up and running again. After that, we'll probably have to split up, as it's hard for four backpackers to get a job at the same place. But it's been fun getting to hang out with my new mates. You'd probably hate it—lots of smelly socks and mess in our room, which is a bit cramped for four of us. It's a bit like being on school camp, except we are bigger and even louder than I remember being when I was at school.

I'd better go. The boys are calling me to come watch a DVD with them. Some boring Christmas film the boss lent us, but I guess it'll help me feel Christmassy and stop me missing you guys.

Say hello to everyone for me!

Aaron

Christmas Disaster

When the residents of Darwin were warned, in the days before Christmas 1974, that a cyclone was coming, many were unconcerned. There had been another cyclone warning only ten days before, and nothing had happened. It was Christmas Eve, and there were presents to wrap and parties to attend.

But this cyclone was different. It was headed for Darwin and, unlike the earlier one, it did not change course. From late on Christmas Eve and into the early hours of Christmas Day, the storm wrought havoc on the city. Wind gusts of 217 kilometres an hour were recorded, but with instruments broken by the wind, it is believed they were even higher. Fierce rain and wind lashed every corner of the city, destroying 70 per cent of the buildings. Seventy-one people were killed, and up to 30,000 people left homeless. Ships were sunk and aircraft were destroyed.

After the cyclone, most of the city's residents were evacuated to other cities around Australia. Many never returned. As buildings were replaced, they had to meet building standards to better withstand future cyclones. The scale of the disaster was unmatched in Australia's history.

Chapter 8

'Come on, Amy, we don't want Mum to miss her plane!' Dad calls.

Don't we? I ask myself. I know I'm being unfair, but I still feel a bit grumpy that Mum is heading off on a trip without me. Everybody has adventures except me. My holidays haven't been very exciting at all. Mum and Dad have both been working, and when she hasn't been working, Mum's been busy getting ready for her trip. Even Trudi has been too busy to hang out much. And besides, I'm going to miss Mum. First Aaron, now her.

Mum comes and stands in the doorway. 'Come on, sweetie. It's time to go!' She's wheeling her suitcase and has her laptop bag over her shoulder. Her face glows with excitement as she jiggles impatiently. It's Mum's first time visiting Europe. She's flying to Paris first, where she'll catch up with Aaron, then catching a train to Brussels and the university where the symposium is.

It all sounds so exciting. I can understand why she's looking forward to it. And it *is* only for a few weeks. I smile back at her, trying not to show my sadness that she's going. 'Sorry, Mum. I'm ready now!'

I quickly close up my own suitcase and grab my backpack. After we drop Mum at the airport, Dad is taking me over to Marysville to stay with Gran. At least I have *something* to look forward to.

The trip to the airport is a lot like the one we did with Aaron only a couple of months ago. Mum and Dad talk about boring stuff like itineraries and research and whatever. I zone out a bit, but then Mum exclaims at something on the radio, and turns it up.

'What—' I start to ask, but Mum shushes me. I remember the climate change expert on the radio last time we went to the airport, and wonder if it's something like that again. Then I realise it's something very different.

'Crossing live to our reporter in New York, Jill Newton,' the voice on the radio says. 'Jill, what can you tell us?'

'Well, Mark,' a female voice begins, 'I'm standing on the banks of the Hudson River in New York. What I'm seeing in front of me is unbelievable. A plane has landed in the river.'

'Landed? Can you tell us what kind of plane?' the man's voice cuts in. In the car, we're all quiet, waiting to hear more. I lean forward to be closer to the radio, my heart sinking. A plane crash!

'Well, Mark,' the woman replies, 'this is no light aircraft. This is a United Airlines passenger jet. Boats are swarming around, choppers are overhead, and the passengers from the flight are being rescued from the wings and the water. It's a surreal sight.'

'Do we know why the plane crashed? Is there any indication of what happened?'

'No, Mark,' the woman replies. 'As you might imagine, it's quite chaotic here. Witnesses, though, are saying that the plane seemed to be coming in to land. This was, it seems, a controlled landing.'

'On a river?' The radio man says what I'm thinking.

'That's what they're saying, Mark. There's no word yet on why the plane landed this way, or even whether there have been injuries or fatalities. For now, as you'd imagine, there's a lot of effort going on out on the water to make sure they save everyone they can.'

The reporter ends the call and the announcer resumes the show. 'We'll try to bring you more details of what's happening there as it comes to hand. But for now, just to repeat, it seems a passenger jet has crash-landed into New York's Hudson River.'

Dad turns the radio down a little. 'Scary stuff!' he says.

My mind races. I remember the plane crashes I've seen on TV so many times, especially the ones from 9/11. 'Do you think it was terrorists?' I ask, trembling. I don't remember 9/11—I was just a baby when that happened. I hope another terrible attack like that one isn't happening right now.

'You heard,' said Dad. 'They really don't know yet.'

Mum has gone quiet. All of the excitement of earlier seems to have drained away. Dad notices too. 'I'm sure it's just an accident,' he says, reaching across to squeeze her shoulder.

What does he mean? It takes me a moment but then I realise what they must be thinking. If bad stuff is happening on planes, is Mum going to be safe? I can't help myself. 'But what if it *is* a terror attack?' I say. 'Maybe you shouldn't be flying, Mum.'

Mum gives me a small smile, turning to look at me. 'It's fine, Amy. It'll be fine. By the time I have to board my plane there will be more information available about what happened.' She puts the end of her thumb in her mouth like she does when she's thinking, chewing at the corner of the nail. 'I'm sure if there's any risk they won't let us fly anywhere, anyway.'

I guess Mum's right, but we're all pretty quiet for the rest of the drive. As we circle the airport carpark though, there's another radio update. 'According to a spokesman, it appears that the plane may have struck a flock of birds shortly after take-off, causing the engines to fail,' the reporter says.

'So there's no indication that this is related to any human activity?' the presenter asks. Maybe he's thinking what I was thinking, about a terrorist attack. He seems to be asking that without using the words.

'Absolutely not,' the woman replies. 'Authorities have stressed that there is no cause for alarm. They are, though, calling it a miracle. That a plane with over 150 passengers on board can crash-land into a busy river, with apparently no fatalities, is a miracle. The pilot is already being called a hero.'

I relax a little. If this was just the result of a freak accident, then Mum will be fine. But then I start to worry again. 'What if something goes wrong with *your* plane?' I ask Mum.

I've never thought about birds hitting planes before.

'Relax,' says Dad, swinging the car into a bay at last. 'She'll be fine, Amy.'

Mum smiles at me as she gets out. 'Of course I'll be okay, darling. People fly safely every day. Actually,' she says, smirking slightly, 'when you think of it, this *is* kind of a natural disaster, like in your book.'

I frown. A plane crash is not a natural disaster.

'You know'—she taps one side of her forehead—'if it was caused by birds, then that's nature at work.'

I giggle a little until I remember that a plane crash is still very serious.

The airport is busy, and it seems that not everyone has heard about the plane crash in America. Either that or they're not worried. Still, after Mum has checked in and we go to sit in a coffee shop, I notice that lots of people are staring at the television screen on the wall. It's showing footage of the rescue. There is no sound coming from the television, so I try to keep up with the subtitles. They are calling the pilot a hero for managing to land the plane without anyone dying.

Mum nudges me. 'There you go, Amy,' she says. 'A hero in the face of a natural disaster.'

I nod. Even though I I'm a bit distracted by the fact that Mum is leaving, I can't wait to learn more about Captain Sullenberger, and how he managed to be so calm and brave. I'm still not convinced it can be called a natural disaster though.

Chapter 9

After we've said goodbye, Mum looking nervous but happy, and me holding back tears, Dad and I drive from the airport straight to Gran's house in Marysville, our second long drive of the day. As we drive through the hills and gullies Dad points out that the bush is much greener than it was a few months ago. 'It's all that rain we had just before Christmas,' he says.

Dad has to slow down all the time, as the corners are very tight. He has his eyes on the road, but I can't help but look up at the gum forest that surrounds us. The trees are amazingly tall, with bare trunks that reach high towards the sky. I can only see tiny patches of blue between them—there are so many, there is barely space between them. At their base are lush green ferns, and it almost looks like their wide leaves are waving at us in the breeze as we pass by.

We've driven this road many times, but I haven't ever taken much notice of what's out the window. Usually everybody is too busy chatting and laughing.

'What sort of trees are these, Dad?'

'Mountain Ash,' Dad says. 'Some of the tallest trees in the country. Over 80 metres tall, some of them.'

Maths isn't my strong subject, but even I know that's higher than a twenty-storey building. 'Wow. That's just …' I can't find the right word so I just say again, 'Wow.'

'Incredible, aren't they? Of course, it takes a long time for them to grow that big,' Dad says. 'Hundreds of years.'

'Right.' I grin. 'So they're about the same age as you, then?'

'Oi, you!' Dad laughs, then he winks. 'Nope, they're a bit younger than me. There used to be a lot more, and some were even over 100 metres, but many of them were cut down.'

'But who would do that?' I couldn't imagine anyone wanting to cut down something so beautiful. 'Why?'

'Oh, the usual reason. Money. People settled around here because of the trees—well, the timber—and then more came in the gold rush.' He looked over at me. 'Industry has its place in the scheme of things, I suppose, but cutting down forests does more than just ruin the view.'

'Mum's always saying deforestation is a huge

contributor to climate change.'

'You sound just like her sometimes, you know. Especially since you wrote that essay.' Dad grinned. 'But the other problem is that logging also leads to more intense bushfires.'

Now I'm confused. 'If there aren't as many trees, how does that work?'

'Older growth forests tend to have wet rainforest growth, but reforested areas have more trees, closer together, with less undergrowth. Lots more fuel, and it's a lot drier. Go on,' he says, pointing out the window. 'Have a good look and you'll see what I mean.'

I let down the window and breathe in the smell of the rainforest floor.

'Good, isn't it?' Dad says. 'Smells even better after the rain.'

'I love that smell,' I say, looking at the little tendrils of fern sprouting not far from the road. 'Petrichor.'

'Yep. That's it. Did Mum tell you that?'

'No, it was Trudi.'

'Well, well,' Dad nods. 'She's a smart one, that Trudi. But,' he adds, 'rain is not always ideal at this time of year, because if there's new growth without much rain afterwards, the ground is dry. That means even more fuel for a fire.'

I remember the rain that fell at the start of the holidays. It's been dry ever since.

Dad glances across. 'Not a very cheery topic, is it?' he says. 'Sorry. I guess in my line of work you can't help spotting risks.' As he reaches to turn the radio back on, he adds, 'hopefully it will never happen.'

'Hopefully,' I agree. I look again at the towering trees, and wonder what animals and birds live here that I can't see from the car.

We arrive at Gran's in the late afternoon. As Dad pulls up in the driveway, Gran comes out the front door and waves madly at us from the veranda. I love Gran's house. It's not as big as the one she and Grandpa had in Canberra, but it feels like she's lived there forever. Mum said it's because she packed up memories and brought them here with her. Every wall, every surface, has something interesting on it, with a story attached. In the spare room, where I'm sleeping, is a bookshelf loaded with photo albums and books Gran has kept since she was my age, even younger. The hallway is lined with lots of family photos, going back to Gran's grandparents, but my favourite is one of Dad, when he was about two, standing in a garden wearing nothing but undies, holding a running hose and laughing as the trickle of water streams down his face. Gran says she wasn't surprised when he became a volunteer firie.

Fire is back in Dad's thoughts the next morning as he pulls the ladder out of Gran's shed and gets to work clearing out her gutters, which she hasn't managed to do.

'These should have been done ages ago, Mum,' he calls down.

'I know,' Gran says, looking up and shaking her head a little. 'And I meant to do it. But time just got away from me.' She watches Dad working up high. 'Oh, Ben. You remind me of your father, seeing you up there.'

She looks a bit sad as she says that. We all miss Grandpa, but of course it's hardest for Gran.

Gran and I get busy raking up the leaves and dirt Dad throws down as he moves around the roof line, and load it into the wheelbarrow.

'Where are we going to put all this?' I ask her when the barrow is nearly full.

Gran sighs. 'I'll just have to pile it up, I think. Usually I'd burn it, but not in the middle of summer.'

'No way!' I say, remembering what Dad said yesterday, and imagining a fire spreading from Gran's yard to the bush surrounding it.

'Compost it, Mum!' Dad calls down.

Gran frowns. 'But it's mostly eucalypt.'

Dad climbs down the ladder, pulling off his gloves and reaching for the water bottle he left on a windowsill. 'Yes,' he says. 'But it's an old wives' tale that you can't compost eucalypt.' He explains that the gum leaves will break down just like the other garden clippings and veggie scraps Gran always adds to her compost bin. 'Oh well, back to work,' he says finally, putting his gloves back on and disappearing back up the ladder.

I grab my new camera and take a few snaps of Dad up the ladder and Gran working in the yard. Then I help Gran shovel the leaves into the bin and spread them out. She nods at the black patch in the corner of her yard close to the back fence.

'Maybe I won't need to use that any more, now that I know,' she says. 'I've been burning leaves when I rake them ever since I got here.'

'Should have asked your clever son!' says Dad, coming down from the ladder again.

'Who? John?' Gran says, smiling cheekily, naming my uncle.

I giggle, and Dad laughs too. 'Guess I walked into that one,' he says. 'But seriously, Mum, the less burning we do the better. It can't be avoided in the forests where we do the controlled burns. And we're kind of doing what the traditional owners did for thousands of years. But here in suburbia, it's best to reuse the plant matter rather than send it all up in flames.'

'Suburbia?' laughs Gran. 'This isn't exactly the suburbs, you know!'

Dad looks around at Gran's yard, filled with mostly native plants, and to the bush beyond. 'I guess not,' he says. 'But you know what I mean.'

'I do,' says Gran. She watches Dad fold the ladder, and we follow him to the shed with the wheelbarrow, rakes and spades. 'Thanks for all your hard work,' she says. 'I feel more fire-ready now.'

I watch Dad give her a hug. 'No worries, Mum,' he says. 'This is a great area to live in, but I do worry about you being so far away from us and the rest of the family. And without Dad ...' His voice trails off.

Gran shrugs. 'I appreciate that,' she says. 'But you do

know I'm okay here, don't you? I might not be a spring chicken, but I'm not exactly old and decrepit either. And I've made lots of new friends here. Besides, you're only half an hour away!'

'True. But after what happened in Canberra—'

Gran frowns. I do too. When she lived in Canberra bushfires came right into the suburbs. Her house was all right, but I know it really scared her and Grandpa. They were luckier than others, but she'd described to me watching the sky turn black, then orange, and having to stamp out flying embers that landed in their garden.

Now Gran gives her head a little shake, as if trying to get rid of a memory. 'I'd rather not think about that. Surely it couldn't happen where I live twice in a lifetime? So don't worry about me.'

'I know, Mum,' says Dad. 'But after all the years you worried about me, John and Ev, it's our turn to worry about you now.'

'Enough worrying!' says Gran. I can see she wants to change the subject. 'Time to fill your stomach instead.'

We all head inside for lunch: chicken and salad sandwiches, followed by some of Gran's scrumptious orange cake. When Dad gets ready to leave, Gran cuts a big slab of the cake and pops it in a container for him to take home. Luckily there's still plenty left for me.

Dear Amy

Thanks for the photos of Dad and Gran. Still no photo of you, but. Are you hiding something? I'll have to check with Mum that you haven't grown an extra nose or something since I left.

I'm writing this quickly because I'm going to catch the Metro to go and meet Mum. The Metro is the underground train system here in Paris. I like it better than the London one—it doesn't seem so cramped.

Have fun staying with Gran. I bet she has you playing Scrabble. You do know you'll never beat her, don't you? She is sooooo good.

Better go. Can't wait to see Mum! Give Gran a hug from me.

Aaron

Chapter 10

'Look, Gran,' I say, pointing at the poster as we park near the supermarket. 'There's something in the paper about that Hudson River plane landing. Can we buy it?'

'Of course! But you'd better let me read the rest of it before you go cutting out the articles about the latest disaster to catch your eye, or your new heroes.'

I grin. I have been known to cut bits out of the paper before people have read them.

We head into the store and, while Gran grabs the milk and flour she came for, I quickly scan the article on the front of the paper.

'I'm going to get this magazine too,' says Gran, coming over to stand beside me. She picks up a travel magazine. 'You can help me make a decision while you're here.'

'What about New York?' I say, pointing to the front cover showing Times Square.

'Who's going to New York?' an old man waiting at the counter says.

Gran gives a funny giggle as she meets the man's

eyes. 'Oh, nobody, Jim. But I'm thinking of doing some travel.'

The man—Jim—smiles and gives Gran a sideways glance. 'Don't go too far away, will you?' he says. 'I might miss you, you know.'

Gran laughs again, shaking her head in amusement. 'Sure, Jim!' she says.

I can feel my mouth hanging open. I think this man is flirting with my gran. And she doesn't seem to mind. I'm not sure how I feel about that.

We put the shopping in the car, then take a stroll down the street. 'Just to stretch my legs,' says Gran, but I know it's also to see if any of her other friends are about. She stops to chat to a lady out working in her garden and waves to a couple who are walking their little dog on the other side of the street.

'That's Joan and Harry,' she tells me. 'They've lived here all their lives.'

Their fluffy white dog runs in front of them sniffing at everything. It's so cute I'd love to pat it. Instead I take a quick photo of it. I'm loving the chance to use my camera.

Marysville is much smaller than Healesville, but I can see why Gran likes it. It feels like its own little world.

There's hardly any traffic because not too many people live here, and there's no passing traffic either. Marysville is right at the bottom of the mountains, and there's a road that heads up into them, and Lake Mountain, so it's probably a bit busier in wintertime than it is now.

But it's not too quiet. Everybody is friendly, and Gran seems to know almost everyone. There's not a lot of shops, but there's some yummy food ones. 'Maybe we should pop into the bakery before we head home?' says Gran, as if she can read my thoughts.

In the end we take our iced buns and go and sit in the park to eat them. I watch some little kids playing on the play equipment.

'You used to love going to parks when you were little,' says Gran.

'Still do,' I say through a mouthful of bun. I might not be climbing on the play equipment, but I'm enjoying sitting with Gran and watching. 'Will we have time to go and visit the falls while I'm here? I'd love to take some photos of it.'

'You bet!' says Gran. I think she loves visiting the big waterfall outside of town as much as I do.

'You going to the falls, Mrs P? When? Can I come?'

A boy I've never seen before appears in front of Gran. I look at him suspiciously. Has he been spying on us?

'Hello to you too, Jackson,' says Gran, but she doesn't sound cross. She smiles at the boy whose face, I decide, looks more pleasant than creepy. He has bright blue eyes, spiky blond hair and a big, friendly smile.

'Yep, that's what I meant to say,' Jackson says to Gran, smiling sheepishly. 'Hello there, Mrs P. Lovely day, isn't it? Now, what were you saying about going to the falls?'

'And what about my guest, Jackson?' she says, gesturing at me. 'This is my granddaughter Amy.'

Jackson looks at me as if he's only just noticed I'm there too, even though he must have known Gran was talking to *me* about the falls. 'Hi, Amy,' he says, smiling. 'Your gran is a very nice person. But she doesn't seem to want to take me to the falls at all.'

I laugh. Jackson is teasing Gran. She laughs too. 'You're kidding, Jackson Edwards! I've taken you there before, haven't I? And, if you're very lucky, Amy might let you come with us tomorrow.'

I hesitate. I don't usually make friends very easily. But Jackson looks at me pleadingly, pretending to beg with his hands clasped together and eyes open wide. I have to laugh. 'Sure. Why not!'

'High five!' Jackson exclaims, holding his hand up for me to slap.

I can't believe I *do* slap it. I've just high-fived a stranger. And a boy!

'You'll have to ask your mum though, Jackson.' She looks at me. 'Would you believe I used to teach Jackson's mum? And now they live just up the street from me!' she explains. 'I've babysat Jackson a few times.'

Jackson blushes. 'Babysat?' he exclaims, his smile slipping a bit. 'I'm not a baby!'

Gran hurries to apologise, realising she has embarrassed Jackson. 'Of course not. We just hang out together, don't we? It's your parents who call it babysitting.' She shrugs. 'I guess us parents never forget that you were once our tiny babies.'

'Don't sweat it, Mrs P,' Jackson says. 'You don't call it babysitting any more, and I won't tell people I'm grannysitting.' The blush has left his face.

Gran nods, laughing. 'Deal!' she says. 'No one grannysits me!'

'I have to go,' says Jackson. 'Mum's cooking a roast

for lunch. But can you let me know about going to the falls?'

'Sure,' says Gran. 'I'll call your mum later.'

'Bye, Mrs P,' says Jackson, walking towards the road. 'Bye, Amy! Nice to meet you!'

I wave and smile to myself. I think I've just made a new friend.

Captain Hero: How Quick Thinking Saved Lives

Aviation Authorities, safety experts and analysts are all applauding the quick thinking and calm demeanour of Captain Chelsea 'Sully' Sullenberger, whose actions in landing a full passenger jet on the Hudson River on Thursday are, they say, nothing but heroic.

Already being dubbed the 'Miracle on the Hudson' by many, the events which unfolded in the skies over New York and, ultimately, the waterways, are capturing attention around the world.

The US Airways flight carrying 155 passengers is

believed to have struck a flock of geese shortly after take-off, damaging both engines. It is believed that the pilot initially planned to return to the airport but, with no power, instead realised he would need to land. And, in the midst of a crowded city, the river appeared his best option.

'I could not believe my eyes,' a witness says. 'I was sitting at my desk on the 20th floor when I saw a plane coming in low over the bridge. I knew it was coming down, but it was slow and controlled like a regular landing. I could not believe what I was seeing.'

The witness called 911, joining hundreds of other callers scrambling to report the landing to authorities.

Passengers aboard the plane say they too were surprised by the landing. 'When the captain said we were going down, I started crying and praying,' a passenger, who did not wish to be named, said on Friday. 'When we landed, I knew we were going to make it. The crew were great—getting us all off. And I believe Captain Sullenberger was the last to leave.'

It has been reported that not only did the man known as Sully land the plane, reports have come in that he then waited until all passengers and crew had left the aircraft before checking the entire plane. 'He wanted to personally be sure no one was left behind,' a source says. 'That man is a hero.'

While the cause of the accident is yet to be known, it seems the world agrees with the source. Captain Sullenberger is a hero.

Chapter 11

'Come on, Amy,' Jackson calls. 'Last one in's a rotten egg!'

'Coming!' I cry, dropping my towel and hurrying to the edge of the pool just as Jackson jumps in.

Splash!

I step back, but not quickly enough, and I'm drenched. 'Hey!' I squeal, shaking water from my face.

Jackson's head pops up from under the water. '*Soorrrry*' he says, but his cheeky smile tells me he doesn't really mean it.

I laugh, and sit on the edge, my feet dangling into the pool. The cool water comes up to my knees.

We've just been for a drive with Gran to visit Steavenson Falls, one of my favourite places in the hills. It's not too far out of town, but standing near the base of the falls, surrounded by trees and ferns, a strip of blue sky up above and the burbling roar of the water cascading over the rocks from above makes you feel like you're miles from everywhere. In spite of the drought, the water still flows pretty strongly, but Gran tells us her friend Bob reckons there's not as much water now as there was before the drought.

I got some great photos, and Jackson and I raced each other up the path to the lookout and then, after we'd got our breath back, back down again.

Jackson won both times.

He also won the rock-skipping contest and the cake-eating contest.

With Jackson, it seems, everything is a contest. But he isn't boastful when he wins.

Like now. Even though he's just beaten me into the pool, he's waiting for me to get in too.

Splash! Water dips off my face.

'Got you!' Jackson says, lowering his hand ready to scoop up another handful.

'Stop it!' I squeal, but I'm laughing.

'Well, come in, then!'

I hesitate. I do love the pool, but I'm not a very good swimmer. What if I go too deep and drown or something? I don't want to tell Jackson I'm not very good.

But his smiling face makes it look like so much fun. Besides, if I don't hurry and get in, he's going to splash me again.

I take a deep breath, counting to three in my head,

and slip in next to him, frantically paddling to stay above the water. My feet search for the bottom.

I can't stand! I move my arms and legs as quickly as I can, but I can feel myself starting to sink. As my face goes under, I get a mouthful of water.

Suddenly a pair of strong hands pushes me in the back, and I realise the edge is within reach.

I grab it, pulling my head above water and leaning onto the side of the pool.

'Are you okay?' I hear Jackson's voice. 'You scared me!'

I take deep, slow breaths. 'I … scared … me … too,' I manage. As the fear starts to leave my body I can feel colour rush to my face. How embarrassing! I nearly drowned in front of Jackson! I sneak a look at him. His smile is gone and his eyes are filled with concern.

'Can't you swim?' he asks, frowning.

I pull myself up to sit back on the edge, shaking my head. 'Only a little bit.' I look at Jackson, still in the water. 'But I just got a bit of a shock—I thought I could stand there.' I look again. Although Jackson's head is above water, he isn't standing—he's treading water. 'I feel so silly!'

'Don't be a numpty,' Jackson says. He's the only person I've ever heard say that, apart from Aaron. 'You don't have to be good at everything. You should see my spelling!' he says.

I smile. I'm sure he's just being nice, but I feel less embarrassed.

I look back to where Gran is sitting in the shade. She's reading a book and doesn't even seem to have noticed what just happened.

'Don't tell Gran,' I say. 'She might not let me come again.'

'Fair enough,' says Jackson, thinking. 'But only if you let me help you learn to swim.' He must see the look of uncertainty on my face. 'Down the shallow end,' he says.

'Deal.' I say.

Chapter 12

'Are you sure you'll be okay?' Gran asks me. 'I can cancel, you know.'

'Don't be silly, Gran. Jackson and me are going to have heaps of fun!'

'Jackson and I,' Gran says, correcting my grammar.

'What, you and Jackson are going somewhere too?' I reply, grinning.

Gran laughs. 'Hey! You've let that Jackson's cheekiness rub off on you.' But she looks pleased rather than cross. She collects her car keys and handbag and heads for the car, waving goodbye to me.

'I have my phone,' she says, 'so get Jackson's mum to call me if there are any problems.'

'It'll be fine, Gran!' I say again. I pick up my backpack and head for the front gate, whistling happily.

Since she moved to Marysville, Gran has taken up playing bridge. She plays every Wednesday with three of her new friends. When I realised she was thinking of cancelling while I was here, I came up with a great idea. She could go and play bridge and I could spend the day hanging out with Jackson. Luckily Jackson and his mum agreed, and Gran looked pleased when she realised she would still get to play bridge.

I head down the quiet street. Gran's house is on the edge of the town—there are probably only about thirty streets in the whole of Marysville—and the top of the rise where Gran's house is feels super quiet sometimes. But it's beautiful, with lots to look at in every direction. There is bush behind her house, and as I walk down the hill I can see the oval and the park at the bottom of the valley.

The houses in Gran's street aren't too close together and each block is filled with more trees and gardens. I wave and call hello to Gran's neighbour, Mrs Simpson, who is out watering her roses.

The ground crunches beneath my feet, but there are few other noises. Except, when I stop to really listen, there's the rustling of leaves in the trees and the sounds of birds.

Another sound breaks the silence. 'Oi! Hurry up, slowcoach!' Jackson is sitting on a tree stump at the end of his driveway. I hurry up the street towards him.

'I thought you'd never get here,' he says.

'Hello to you too,' I say, smiling. It feels a bit funny to be back-chatting a boy in such a friendly way. All my other friends are girls. I wonder what Trudi will say when I tell her about Jackson.

'What do you want to do first?' Jackson asks.

'Are you hungry?' I ask, knowing even as the words leave my mouth what the answer will be. Jackson is always hungry.

I'm right. He nods enthusiastically.

'Gran gave me some money, so we can go to the bakery. Or the lolly shop.'

'Let's do both!' Jackson says. 'We can have a picnic in the park. And then maybe a swim at the pool.'

We head inside to check out plans with his mum and soon, with our swimming things in our backpacks, and sunscreen applied, we're heading towards the main street.

It seems like Jackson knows everyone in town. An old lady waves from behind her picket fence where she's checking her letterbox, a couple of little kids call out from their front veranda as we pass, and even a cat comes out from a front yard to rub around Jackson's feet.

'Hello, Toulouse,' Jackson says as he bends to scratch

the ginger cat's ears. When I bend to pat it too, it looks at me a bit warily but then seems to decide I must be okay, and lets me stroke him.

Finally we start walking again and reach the bakery. I buy a sausage roll and a jam and cream doughnut and Jackson chooses a sausage roll and a chocolate éclair. Then we head to the lolly shop.

The choices there are even harder, but luckily we can get small amounts of lots of different lollies. There are so many to choose from!

We head to the park and find a shady bench, and then we eat every last bite. It is so good!

'I'm full!' I say at last. 'I don't think I'll ever eat anything again.'

'Me too,' said Jackson. 'I won't be able to eat for like—' He looks at his watch. 'Ten minutes.'

'Ten minutes?' I groan, clutching my full tummy. Then I remember this is Jackson speaking. Ten minutes without eating might be a lot for him. Then I look at him and realise he's laughing.

'Hey, Jackson!' a voice calls out.

Three kids I haven't seen before are heading towards us—two boys and a girl, about our age. 'Who's your friend?' one of the boys asks.

Some of my happiness drains away. Strange kids. Are they going to like me?

'Hi, guys,' Jackson says. 'This is Amy.'

He introduces me to his friends. Nathan, the boy who's done all the talking till now, looks me up and down but smiles. The other boy, Vin, does too. The girl, Tasha, gives me a long look but then she grins too. Relief washes over me.

'Watcha up to?' Nathan asks.

'Just hanging around,' Jackson says. 'Amy's from Healesville but she's staying here for a couple of weeks with her gran, Mrs P.'

'Ohhhhh,' Tasha says. 'Cool.' Her smile is wider now. Maybe she likes my gran.

'We're going to head to the pool later,' Jackson says. 'But we've just had a pig out so might have to let the food settle first.'

'Come play cricket?' Vin asks, holding up the bat he's been carrying.

Jackson jumps up, keen, but then seems to remember that I'm there. 'You wanna?' he asks me.

I'm not super keen. I haven't played cricket much,

except in sport at school. But I can see that Jackson wants to, so I nod and try to look enthusiastic.

We cross the park to the oval, and soon I'm so busy chasing the ball and throwing, and even catching, that I forget I don't like cricket. Jackson's friends seem happy to have an extra player.

Later, hot from all the exercise, we head over to the pool. The others drop their towels and jump straight in, but I feel suddenly shy. What if they're all much better swimmers than me? Only Jackson knows that I'm not very good.

Jackson catches my eye and gives a half smile, which I think means he knows what I'm thinking.

'Let's play Marco Polo,' he says, heading for the shallow part of the pool.

I give him a grateful smile and soon the five of us are splashing and playing and no one seems to notice that I don't go where I can't stand.

Later I sit on my towel and watch the three boys horsing around, splashing each other and play fighting. They seem to have more energy than me. I'm a bit tired.

Tasha comes to sit with me.

'So,' she asks, giving me a sideways look, 'are you

Jackson's girlfriend?'

I feel colour flood my face and I don't know what to say. I think Jackson is just my friend, who happens to be a boy. But I've never really had a good friend who's a boy before.

'I …' I say, but can't think what else to say.

'It's okay if you are,' Tasha says. 'I used to like him but now I like Vin.' She thinks for a moment. 'But Jackson is pretty cute, don't you think?'

I look at him in the pool. Right now he's grimacing in mock horror as he play fights Vin. And I know just what to say. 'With that face?' I ask, and I laugh.

Tasha laughs too, and luckily doesn't ask any more., though later, when the boys join us I see her watching Jackson and me closely. I can't decide if she's jealous or just curious.

Jackson looks at his watch. 'We should go, Amy,' he says. 'I told Mum we'd be home by three.'

I can't believe it's three o'clock already. It was ten when we left Jackson's, but we've been so busy having fun that I didn't notice time passing.

As we trudge back up the hill to Jackson's house, my tummy rumbles. 'We missed lunch!' I say, surprised.

Jackson looks surprised too. 'So we did! Unless you count sausage rolls?'

'And the chocolate éclair—' I say.

'And the doughnut,' he adds.

'And the lollies,' we both say at the same time, before looking at each other and laughing.

When we get to Jackson's we're both happy to see a plate of freshly cut watermelon on the kitchen table. It's the perfect thing after our hot walk home. This has been such a great day. It's a shame it has to end, but eventually Gran comes to pick me up.

'Pool tomorrow?' Jackson asks as we say goodbye.

'Sure thing!' I say.

Gran lifts an eyebrow. 'Hmm. I thought you came to spend time with me,' she laughs.

'That's okay, Mrs P,' Jackson says. 'You can come too if you like.'

Gran looks from Jackson to me and back again. 'We'll see,' she says.

Hi Mum

Thanks for sending the photos. It looks like you and Aaron had a great time in Paris. Did you climb to the top of the

Eiffel Tower?

Guess what? Gran has booked a trip to Paris too. She had almost decided to go to New York and then she saw your photos of Paris and told me she used to have a penpal in France when she was a teenager. She found an old letter from her, in a box in her shed, and showed me. So now she's writing to her old friend Marie to see if she's still there. I'm so excited for her that I hardly feel jealous. It must be a bit lonely for her after Grandpa dying. Although not while I'm around!

I have a new friend too. A boy named Jackson who lives just down the road. Gran knows his mum. He came with us to visit the falls, and we went to the pool a few times too. He even helped me learn to swim a bit better. I swam freestyle right across the Marysville pool.

Dad is coming to pick me up today. Only two sleeps and then the holidays are over. I'm excited to start Year Six but I'm going to miss it here, I've had such a good time. Yesterday, for my last day here, Gran took me on a bushwalk to see the 'Big Tree', which is 400 years old and 85 metres tall (I read that on the sign—I didn't measure it myself!). Dad taught me quite a bit about trees on the way up here, you will be glad to know. And we saw Big Culvert, the really old bridge. Gran said it might not be the Eiffel Tower, or the Pont Neuf, but we have lots of beautiful things in our own backyard. Amazing that we've lived in Healesville so long but never been to these places. Did you know they were there?

Hope you got to Brussels okay and that your meetings go well. I'm attaching a photo I took at Steavenson Falls. The boy next to Gran pulling a silly face is Jackson.

Miss you heaps.

Amy

Chapter 13

'So what did you get up to on the holidays?' Trudi asks as we sit under a tree in the playground. 'We hardly saw each other.'

'I know,' I say. 'But I had to go and stay with my gran.' I tell her about Scrabble, and Steavenson Falls and wonder what I should tell her about Jackson. Not that I really want to keep secrets from Trudi. I just don't know how to talk abut it. I'm just about to mention him when Trudi changes the subject.

'It's *soooo* hot,' she moans. 'Pretty sure I'm melting.' She throws her head back, looking longingly up at the tree, as if she hopes it will somehow give us extra shade.

'Me too.' I take a deep gulp from my drink bottle, but the water isn't refreshing. It's warm. 'We shouldn't have to come to school when it's like this.'

It's only the first day of school and already we're sick of it. It's hot, and the work is hard, even on the first day. The only good thing is that we get to see each other again.

'At least we're still in the same class as each other,' says Trudi, brightening up a little. 'Poor Jess and Shae, being split up.'

'Yeah. And Shae has to sit next to Leith too.' I shudder. I still haven't forgiven Leith for being so mean after the spider incident last year. And he's in my class again this year.

'At least Shae's under the fan,' says Trudi. 'My seat is the hottest in the room.'

I'm not convinced that's true, but I don't say so. The whole classroom is like an oven. The weather, which was pretty mild on the holidays, has decided that back-to-school week is the best time to turn up the heat.

The day drags by, but at last the bell rings and, even better, there's a surprise for us. When Trudi's mum picks us up, she doesn't take us straight home.

'We're off to the pool,' she says. 'I've got your bathers in the boot.'

'High five!' Trudi says, turning to me in the back seat. 'We thought we were going to melt today!'

The pool is crowded. There are kids doing after-school swimming lessons and swimming squads training in some of the lanes. And, of course, kids like us who just want to cool down a bit. After we've changed into our bathers we head to the leisure pool and leap in.

'Aaaaah,' I sigh, coming up from my dive and paddling to the side of the pool. 'That's better.' The water isn't exactly ice-cold, but it's so much cooler than the air outside.

'You can dive now!' Trudi exclaims.

'Yes,' I say, smiling proudly, as I hold on to the edge. 'And swim a bit better too.' I realise I still haven't told her about Jackson. 'A kid I met in Marysville helped me.'

'A kid?' Trudi looks at me suspiciously. She's noticed that I was careful not to say 'boy'. 'Who?'

I giggle, realising I'm going to have to finally tell her. 'Okay, a boy. Jackson.' Why am I blushing? 'But it wasn't like that!' I add, as Trudi whistles.

'*Suuuure*,' says Trudi, then teases, 'Amy's got a boyfriend!'

I giggle and splash her. 'No way!' I say. 'He's just a friend.'

'A really good friend.' Trudi laughs.

'Not as good as you,' I reassure her. I want to change the subject before she teases me some more. I look around.

'Hey, there's Jess and Shae,' I say, pointing across the pool where I've just spotted our friends. 'Race you!'

We splash and dash our way over to them, and soon we're playing pool chasey. This is so much more fun than being stuck in a hot classroom.

Eventually, though, we get sick of chasing, and just sit in the shallow water near the toddler area, enjoying the cool and watching groups of kids swimming and playing all around the aquatic centre.

'Are we doing swimming lessons at school this term?' Shae asks.

Secretly I hope not, even though the others are pretty enthusiastic. Staying cool is brilliant, but I'm always in the bottom class at swimming lessons. Even after Jackson's help, I'm still not as good as my friends. Just another thing I'm not very good at.

While the other girls talk and laugh, my mood has changed. I wonder if I'll ever find the thing that I'm good at.

We haven't got any homework, so later at home I flick through *Hard Times: Australia's Worst Natural Disasters*, looking for a page I remember.

'Hey, Dad, did you know that during a big flood in Brisbane, a politician jumped into the floodwaters to try to save some soldiers?' I ask.

Dad looks up from the book he's reading. 'A politician?' he asks. 'Are you sure?'

I read some more, checking the facts. 'Yes. His name was Bill Lickiss.' I read the story again. 'There were live power lines in the water too. He could have been electrocuted!'

Dad looks impressed. 'That's pretty amazing,' he says. 'Bravest thing I've heard a politician do.'

I think so too. He didn't have to do that—he could have just stayed in his big important office.

So many heroes who have achieved amazing things or survived terrible ordeals! It's incredible, especially considering I get nervous about even basic everyday things like swimming or speaking at assembly. I sigh.

Dad hears my sigh. 'What's the matter, Amester. Missing Mum?'

'I guess,' I say, closing my book. But maybe I should tell him what's really bugging me. 'I was just thinking about all these people, overcoming terrible natural disasters, even saving other people's lives! How do they get like that?'

Dad shrugs. 'I don't know,' he says, then thinks for a moment. 'I'm not even sure if some people are actually braver than other people.'

'You're kidding!' I say, pointing at my book. 'There are people in here who've done amazing things. Like—'

Dad shrugs. 'Of course,' he says. 'There are people who do really courageous things, like your politician—'

'Bill Lickiss,' I interrupt.

'Or even Captain Sully.'

I nod.

'But,' Dad says, 'are they brave first, or are they faced with stuff that helps them find that bravery already inside them?'

I feel my nose wrinkle the way it does when I'm confused. 'What do you mean?'

'Well,' Dad says, 'maybe all of us are brave on the inside. But on a normal day we don't need to use that bravery for big things, so instead we just do the things we need to do, like go to work, or cook dinner …'

'Or go to school?' I ask.

'Exactly!' Dad says. 'For most of us, no special bravery required. But then, if something big happens, like a plane crash or a flood or whatever, we do what needs to be done. What we have to do to survive.'

I kind of get what Dad's saying, but I'm not sure I

buy it. 'So you're saying anyone could do what Sully did and land a plane on a river?'

Dad laughs. 'Not exactly. You'd have to be a trained pilot, for a start.'

I nod.

'But on the day, Sully did what needed to be done. He didn't have time to panic or to wonder why him or any of that stuff. That bravery was hidden somewhere inside him. Same with your flood guy, and your other heroes.' He points at my book.

'Maybe,' I say. 'But I don't think I have any of that hidden inside me. I'm scared of everything. I think in an emergency I would just want to hide.'

Dad puts his hand on my shoulder. 'Don't be so hard on yourself, Amy. What I'm saying is, everyone's scared of stuff. I worry about losing you or Mum or Aaron. I'm scared of going to the dentist.' This surprises me. 'But I go anyway, because I can't stand toothache. And I'm scared of fire.'

'Of fire?' I say, amazed. 'But you're a volunteer firefighter!'

'Yes,' says Dad. 'Which means I see first hand just how vicious fires can be. They move fast, they're unpredictable, and they're very hard to stop, especially out in the bush. So of course I'm scared.'

'So how do you keep doing it?' I ask, puzzled. 'If I was you I'd stay home when the pager goes off.'

Dad shakes his head. 'I use what I know.' He sees that I don't understand. 'I've trained to fight fires. I know how to use the tools at my disposal, to work as a team, and to follow instructions. And I know what to do if things don't go to plan.'

I don't ask him what this means—I'm not ready to think about Dad in trouble in the middle of a fire.

'So I use that fear,' Dad continues.

'What do you mean, "use" it?' I ask. What good is fear?'

'Because I'm wary, I don't do anything stupid. No unnecessary risks.' He sits back in his chair a little, watching to see if understand.

I nod, thinking about what he has said. 'Well, that's very brave of you, Dad. But I'm not like that. I'm afraid of so much, and I don't know how to use my fear at all.'

Dad reaches over and gives my shoulder a squeeze. 'Don't be so sure of that,' he says. 'I think you're brave in ways you don't even realise.'

I wait for him to go on, wondering if he's got a good example.

'You're brave enough to eat my cooking, for example.'

I laugh. Dad managed to burn the pasta sauce tonight, but we still choked it down. Maybe that *was* brave.

'Now,' says Dad, 'I think it's time for bed.' He reaches over and gives me a hug. 'Goodnight, my brave Amy.'

The talk has made me feel a little bit better. Maybe I can use that hidden bravery to get through swimming lessons.

High Water

The Brisbane River runs through the city of Brisbane, providing transport and beautiful scenery. But when it floods, as it did in 1974, there can be terrible consequences.

The flood, in late January, was the result of a very wet spring in Queensland. Since October the rivers had been full, but the rain did not stop coming. When Cyclone Wanda hit the state, disaster struck. The cyclone itself was not a big one, but it brought torrential rain—over 600 millimetres in less than two days on the Australia Day long weekend. The already full rivers could not cope.

The levels in the Brisbane River rose rapidly, and it broke its banks. The peak level was measured at 5.5 metres. Buildings in the central city and numerous suburbs were affected. 8500 houses were flooded and most of these were destroyed. Sixteen people drowned, including two soldiers who were thrown into the river when their vehicle hit submerged power lines. With electricity still live, politician Bill Lickiss risked his own life jumping into the water to try to save one of the soldiers.

The aftermath of the flood was massive. As well as the deaths, many people were left homeless, and the financial cost of the flood was close to one billion dollars.

Dear Amy

Thanks for your emails. Sorry I've been slow replying. I had a busy week with Mum. She's headed off to Brussels now.

It was cool having Mum around, even if a bit weird after not seeing anyone from home for so long. We did lots of touristy stuff—lucky for me Mum was paying, as it can get a bit expensive.

I managed to convince Mum to climb up the Eiffel Tower with me. She wasn't too keen at first, reckoned she was just as happy to see it from the outside, but I told her she couldn't come to Paris and not do it. I even offered to hold her hand if she got scared. You know she doesn't like heights very much. But in the end she loved it.

I didn't know before we went, but the tower only has three floors, and the stairs only go to the first two. You have to get an elevator to the top floor. So we climbed the stairs for the first two—once I realised there was a lift, I suggested to Mum we take that the whole way, but she reckoned I was being lazy. So we walked a gazillion steps, admired the view from the second floor, then caught the lift to the top floor. Wow. What an amazing view. It felt like we could see all of France! Get Mum to show you the photos—and keep an eye on the letterbox for the postcard we sent.

My new mate Joel and I are heading to Italy tomorrow. My money is getting low, so if I don't find work I won't stay very long. I'll head back to England and try to get some more work there. I don't want to spend all my money and have to come home too soon.

But I miss you and Dad. And Gran. Sounds like you had a great time staying with her. And her trip sounds ace. Hopefully I'll still be in Europe when she comes, and I can catch up with her. Do you reckon I could get her to climb the Eiffel Tower?

Enjoy being back at school. Remember only six more years and you'll be free!

Love

Aaron

Chapter 14

'It's *sooooo* hot,' I moan to Trudi for the umpteenth time. 'I wish it would *raaaaaain*.'

Trudi nods, but then smirks at me. 'Remember how grumpy you were about the rain at the start of the Christmas holidays? You were all like "it's not *faaaaaiiiiiiirr*. I want to go to the *poooool*". She grins as she tries to impersonate me. I don't tell her, but she does sound a bit like me.

'Me?' I say, trying to look innocent as I remember all too well complaining about the rain stopping me from having fun. 'Are you sure?'

Trudi gives my arm a light punch. 'Definitely! Maybe it's your fault that it hasn't rained since. Haven't you ever heard the saying about being careful what you wish for? My mum says that all the time.'

I shake my head. 'Pretty sure I'm not powerful enough to change the weather.' I think for a moment. 'If I was, I'd be changing it back right this second!'

'I wish!' says Trudi.

When the bell rings to go back into class, for once

we don't mind. At least there are fans in the classroom.

On the way in though, something flies into my face, and I squeal and jump back.

'What happened?' asks Trudi.

I blink, watching the thing fly away. It's just a big fly, I realise, my heart pounding anyway. I'm just about to tell Trudi what it was, but I see Leith watching, a little smile on his mouth.

'Nothing,' I say, trying to look as if nothing just happened. The last thing I want is to let Leith hear me say I was scared by a fly! If he teased me for a week about a spider last year, how much more would he tease me for squealing at a fly?

The afternoon drags by, but when I get home, there's a surprise waiting for me. Gran's little blue car is parked in the driveway.

'Gran!' I call when I open the door, smiling as she appears from the lounge room. 'What are you doing here? I didn't know you were coming!'

'Neither did I until this morning,' Gran says, giving me a big hug. 'But your dad rang and asked me to come over for a night or two.'

I frown. 'Why? Is he hoping you'll cook some better

meals?' I smile, thinking of the pretty average meals we've had lately. Dad and Mum have always shared the housework, but Dad has never been any good at cooking. He even burns toast.

Gran laughs. 'No.' She thinks for a moment. 'Well, maybe,' she says, 'but that's not why he asked me to come. He's been called out to fight a fire and he's likely to be late home. If he comes home at all.'

'A fire?' I say. 'Where abouts?'

'In the Bunyip National Park, down the other side of Melbourne, but they've called in extra staff to help. I was just looking for updates online.' She heads back into the lounge room and I follow. 'Seems there's a few fires around.' She points at the website she has open. 'This blinkin' hot weather!'

'I wish it would rain!' I say, repeating what I said earlier to Trudi.

'Don't we all?' says Gran, turning to shut down the computer. 'I've even been running my air conditioner at home—which you know I hate to do. Speaking of which—' she gets up from her chair and crosses over to the air conditioning unit on the wall of the lounge room, jabbing the temperature button, 'this one doesn't seem to be doing much, does it?'

She's right. Even though air blows out the front vents of the unit, it doesn't seem any cooler than the air around it. I hold my hand in front of it for a moment, hoping it will get cooler, but it doesn't.

'Never mind,' says Gran. 'Let's have a cold drink instead.'

We head for the kitchen where Gran has a jug of homemade lemon squash in the fridge. She pours us each a glass, the ice cubes clinking as she pours.

'Here's to cooler weather,' she says, holding up her glass.

'And no fires,' I add, holding up my own before taking a big sip. Gran's lemon squash is delicious—sweet, tangy and also wonderfully cool.

Gran nods. 'Definitely no fires,' she agrees, pausing to sip from her own glass. 'But it *is* lovely to have an excuse to visit my favourite granddaughter.'

I smile, even though I know she's only saying that because I'm her only granddaughter. All my cousins are boys.

Dear Mum

I hope you're enjoying Brussels. I looked at the weather forecast for there and it sounds freezing. I hope all those layers of clothing you took are doing their job and keeping you warm.

Funny to think of you being freezing and us here at home practically melting. It has been hot for days and days. The first couple of days back at school the temperature was way over 40 degrees. That is soooo hot.

Worse than that, there are lots of fires, and Dad has been busy helping fight some of them. I don't know if he told you, but he got Gran to come and stay with us so that I'm not alone. I'm glad he did because he's hardly been home at all the last three days. The fires are a long way from us, but I'm sure I can smell smoke, especially at night. I hope they get them under control soon.

Gran and I are having a good time. In the evenings we've been playing Scrabble or watching TV. And trying to think up ways of getting cool. The air conditioner in the lounge room doesn't seem to be working at all. I felt sorry for Gran—stuck in the hot house all day while I'm at school—but instead of staying home, she's been visiting the library and going to the shops—anywhere there is air conditioning. Smart cookie. And, luckily, a much better cook than Dad.

Miss you heaps.

Amy

Chapter 15

In my dream I'm in the kitchen and the oven door is open, even though there's a roast dinner cooking inside. Heat from the oven flows around the room, and I can feel beads of sweat on my forehead. 'Can't we close the oven?' I ask Gran. 'It's just too hot.'

Gran laughs. 'Close the oven, Amy? That would never do!' Instead she reaches over and turns the temperature up. The meat in the pan sizzles loudly and waves of heat hit me.

'*Noooo*,' I moan, backing away towards the back door. 'It's *tooo* hot, Gran!' Why is she insisting on making the house hotter?

'Amy!' Gran's voice rouses me from the dream. 'Wake up!'

I groan and roll over, glad to realise that it was just a dream. But even though I'm awake and in my bedroom, instead of the kitchen, I'm still hot and sweaty. That part of my dream was totally real. I can see why I was dreaming about ovens.

I stumble out of bed and to the bathroom. I turn

the cold tap in the shower and stand under it for a few moments, till I'm shivering. The relief is bliss.

Although we had a few days where the temperature dropped a bit, it has been hot all week. It did get down into the 30s, but that is still stupidly hot. And the air conditioner still isn't working. By the time I've pulled on my school uniform and trudged to the kitchen for breakfast I'm hot again, as if the cold shower was just part of my dream too. I wish I could go back to the bathroom and stand under the stream of cold water, clothes and all.

'Why the long face?' asks Gran, handing me a plate of toast.

'Thanks, Gran,' I mumble, reaching for the butter. 'I'm just tired. And hot.' I'm also missing Mum, but I don't say that out loud.

Gran smiles sympathetically. 'Didn't sleep well, huh?' She hands me the strawberry jam and watches as I spread it thickly on my toast. 'Hopefully this weather changes soon.'

'Is Dad up?' I ask. We've hardly seen Dad all week. The fires have kept him busy and he's only come home to eat and sleep. Last night he didn't get home till after I was in bed.

'Gone already,' says Gran through a mouthful of toast. She pours me a glass of orange juice and passes it across the table.

'Already?' I ask, taking the juice. 'But it was so late when he came in last night.'

'Did he wake you?' asks Gran, looking concerned.

'Not really,' I say, swallowing my mouthful of toast. 'I just heard his car pull in.' I'm surprised I didn't also hear him leave this morning. Maybe I did get more sleep than I realise.

I wonder how much sleep Dad had. Not much if he's up and gone already.

'What if he's too tired to fight the fires?' I ask Gran, thinking about the chat Dad and I had last week about him keeping safe. 'He needs to be alert in case of danger.'

Gran smiles reassuringly. 'I know,' she says. 'But I'm sure he knows what he's doing. And the fire controllers do keep track of everyone and make sure they have rest breaks, and food and water.' She pats my hand as she gets up from the table. 'Do try not to worry, Amy.'

I know she means well, but how am I supposed not to worry about my dad when he's off fighting fires?

'I'll drive you to school again,' Gran says, when I

push my plate away. I've only eaten half my toast. 'It's far too hot to walk.'

'Too hot for anything,' I moan. 'Especially school!'

'Maybe,' she says, looking sympathetic. 'But it isn't like you're going to get cool here, with the air conditioner broken.'

'You're right, I guess,' I sigh. 'At least there's fans at school. But when is it going to get cooler?'

It's Gran's turn to sigh. 'Not any time soon.' She points at the newspaper on the kitchen table, open at the weather page. 'They're forecasting a really hot weekend. Record temperatures even.'

As we get ready to leave, I glare at the air conditioner on the lounge room wall. 'Did Dad have time to see about getting that fixed?'

Gran shakes her head. 'I'm going to call the repair people again today, but I don't hold out much hope. When I rang the other day they were booked solid until next week.'

At least the car is cooler. Gran turns the aircon on and it blows delicious cold air over us as we drive to school. 'Could we sit in the car all weekend?' I ask hopefully. I picture us driving around being icy cool instead of cooped up in our oven-like house.

Gran shakes her head. 'No. But maybe, if your dad agrees, we could head back to my place. My air conditioner is still working—I hope—and it would give me a chance to check my mail and water my garden.'

'Let's do it!' I say. 'Anything to cool down a bit.' Thinking of being cool gives me another idea, as I think of the Marysville swimming pool. 'Maybe we could even head to the pool? I bet Jackson would come with us!' I make a mental note to email Jackson if Dad says we can go. It would be great to hang out with him again.

Gran nods. 'Good plan. But I'll have to check with your dad. He might like to spend some time with us on the weekend.'

I hadn't thought of that. 'Maybe,' I say, thinking quickly. 'If he has the weekend off, he could come too though.'

As it turns out, Dad thinks Gran's idea is a good one. With several fires still burning, and the fire danger being extreme, he's going to have a busy weekend. When I get back from school he's at home, but he tells me he could get called back to work at any time.

'Just be aware,' he says to Gran, 'that the forecast

for the weekend is terrible. The whole state is on alert for extreme fire danger.' He looks thoughtful, scratching at the stubble on his chin. I guess he hasn't had much time to shave. 'Actually,' he says, 'maybe going back to Marysville isn't such a good idea. What if there's a fire there?'

Gran smiles and pats him on the shoulder. 'We'll be fine,' she says. 'I'm fire ready, thanks to the help you gave me clearing the gutters. The garden is trimmed and my fire kit is always in the front hall in the summer. We'll be fine.' She looks thoughtful. 'You do know that there's just as much chance of a fire hitting Healesville as Marysville, don't you?'

I know she's thinking of the fires that hit Canberra when she and Grandpa lived there. No one expected back then that a bushfire would come right into the suburbs.

'I guess,' he says. 'But you will be careful, won't you? And if there any fires here in the hills, I want you to leave early. Don't come back here—head into Melbourne to John or Ev's place.'

Gran pats him on the shoulder again. 'We'll do that, I promise. Now try not to worry about us. In fact'—she points a finger at him—'it's us who should be worried about you. You're the one putting yourself in danger fighting fires!'

Dad shakes his head. 'I hadn't thought of that. But you must know we do everything we can to stay safe.' He gives me a little smile, and I know he's thinking about our conversation.

'And so will we,' says Gran. 'Now we'd better go so we can get there before dinner time—and so you can get some rest. No, don't get up,' she says as Dad starts to get up from his lounge chair. 'You must be exhausted.'

It's true. Dad looks really tired. I give him a hug and kiss his bristly cheek. 'Gran's right,' I say. 'Get some rest, Dad. You look after yourself, and Gran and I will look after each other.'

Dad smiles and waves tiredly as we head out to the car. He'll probably be asleep before we've got onto the main road.

In the car, I can't stop thinking about what Gran said to Dad. Until last week, I'd never really thought about him helping fight fires as something dangerous. It's just something he's always done as part of his job and as a volunteer.

'Gran?' I ask. 'Do you really think Dad is in danger

when he works with the fire crews?'

Gran sighs, giving me a sideways glance as she steers the car into the traffic. 'Yes,' she says finally. 'I do. But'—she reaches her free hand over and gives my knee a little squeeze—'I don't want you worrying about him.'

How can I not worry? I don't want Dad to be in danger. But I wait to see what else Gran has to say.

'But I also trust that he will do everything he can to stay safe. He won't take any unnecessary risks.'

She waits for me to say something, but my mind is still working overtime trying to figure out why Dad would fight fires if it's dangerous.

Finally Gran speaks again, and it's as if she's been reading my mind. 'It's a brave thing they do, firefighters and parks officers like your dad.' She pauses, looking to her right as she waits to turn. 'But it's important work. When they work hard to fight a fire, they save bushland. They stop forests and animal habitats being destroyed. And sometimes they're saving lives too, keeping the fires away from houses and towns. They're heroes.'

Heroes! I had never thought of Dad as a hero. But hearing Gran talk, I know she's right.

'Maybe Dad should get a medal,' I say. I think about

the conversation Dad and I had about bravery, and this makes me remember something. 'Did you know Dad is scared of fires? He told me.'

Gran shrugs a little without taking her hands off the steering wheel. 'No. He's never told me that,' she says finally. 'But it doesn't surprise me. Being brave doesn't mean not being scared of things. An out-of-control fire is a pretty scary thing.' I see her shudder. When the fire hit Canberra, it got pretty close to her and Grandpa's house. I guess she's remembering that day. 'But brave people are the ones who use their fear to make sensible decisions. To confront the problem without taking stupid risks.' She glances over to see if I'm still listening. 'In the case of firefighting, I guess they have to know when to keep fighting it and when to withdraw. And they have to listen to the people giving orders. And trust each other and their equipment.'

That sounds a lot like what Dad said. I think about it all for a minute. 'I don't think I'd ever be brave enough to be a firefighter.'

Gran smiles, squeezing my knee again. 'You're braver than you think, Amy,' she says. 'But that doesn't mean you have to go and become a firefighter.'

I grunt. 'I think I'll be something safer. Like a lion tamer.'

Gran frowns, then sees my grin and realises I'm joking. 'Or a snake charmer?' she asks, catching on.

I giggle. 'Or a tightrope walker.'

We both laugh as we try to think of crazier and more dangerous jobs that I could do. The drive over to Marysville seems to fly by as we talk and laugh the whole way.

Dear Aaron

You are so lucky being in Europe. I bet it's really cold there. It's boiling hot here at the moment. Over 40 degrees! The Premier has been warning everyone that the fire danger is extreme, and that we should expect bad fires this weekend. I hope he's wrong, but Dad has been working extra time all week helping with fires already burning in the state forests. He's hardly been home all week.

Gran came to stay with me, but we are in Marysville tonight. The air conditioner at home is broken, so right now we're in her lounge room with the air conditioner turned up—even though it's night time. I usually love summer, but this is just too much. Hopefully Gran will take me and my new friend Jackson to the pool—and we can try to cool down a bit!

Are you still in Italy? And does it snow there? And if so, can you send me a snowball attached to your next email? LOL.

Gotta go. Gran is dishing up two big bowls of ice cream. Better eat it before it melts!

Miss you heaps.

Amy

Chapter 16

'We're fine,' I hear Gran say as I struggle to open my eyes, wondering who she's talking to. 'There are no fires near us, and I'll keep an eye on the website, and the radio on. At the first sign of trouble, we'll head into Melbourne.' She pauses, and I realise she must be on the phone. 'I promise. Now you get back to work and keep yourself safe too. I love you.'

I hear the beep as she hangs up and then her footsteps as she comes closer down the hall.

'Good morning, Gran,' I call.

'Oh,' Gran replies, poking her head through the door to my room. 'Sleeping beauty awakes! I thought you were going to sleep all day.'

I stretch again, grinning. 'What time is it?' I ask.

'Just after nine o'clock,' Gran says. 'You must have been tired.'

Nine o'clock! I never sleep that late. Aaron does, but not me. Even on weekends I'm always up by eight.

I spring out of bed. 'You should have woken me!' I say to Gran.

'Nah.' Gran smiles. 'You looked so sweet fast asleep. But I'm glad you're awake now. Jackson will be here soon.'

'Jackson?' I jump out of bed. 'Cool!'

'His parents are going into Healesville for the day, but he didn't want to go. So Gina texted to see if he could come and see you instead.'

'Cool!' I say again. Jackson must have got the email I sent him last night telling him I was here.

'No, not cool, hot! ' Gran says, wiping a hand across her brow. 'Far too hot to do anything much, so we'll have to find something inside you two can do.' She spots my bathers poking out of my overnight bag. 'But maybe later I can take you both to the pool.'

'Yes!' That's what I'd been hoping she'd say.

Gran's right. It is super hot. My nightie sticks to my skin and, although the curtains are drawn tightly on the bedroom window, I can feel the heat coming through the glass.

'It's already over 40 degrees outside,' says Gran. 'And it's going to get hotter still.'

'That's ridiculous!' I say. 'We'll melt!'

Gran sighs. 'It's terrible,' she agrees. 'There are more fires starting, and the radio says it's going to get worse.'

I remember the phone call I heard when I woke up. 'Was that Dad on the phone?' I ask.

Gran nods. Apparently Dad was ringing before he went back on duty. 'He wanted to check we're okay,' Gran says. 'I promised we'd start going through my fire plan.'

Gran has mentioned her fire plan before, but I've never asked exactly what that is. Soon though, I'm helping with the tasks. And when Jackson arrives, he helps too.

First we collect all the items on Gran's checklist and pack them into a bag near the front door. There's a torch, Gran's spare radio, and two big bottles of water as well as two folders full of Gran's important documents.

'Add this to the pile, Amy,' Gran says, handing me a woollen blanket.

It's so hot I can't see why she'd need a blanket, but I don't argue. I'm sure there's a reason why it's on the fire checklist.

Next Gran packs a change of clothes and extra underwear and tells me to do the same. My bag is mostly still packed from last night, so I hand it to Jackson to add to the pile near the door. I blush when I realise one of my pairs of undies is right on top where he can see it, but he doesn't say anything as I quickly close the zip.

'And my mobile phone charger,' says Gran, putting her phone in her back pocket and adding the charger to her bag.

With everything packed neatly, she sends me to get her set of keys.

'Put them into the front door, please,' she says.

'But the door isn't locked,' I say, puzzled.

'That's okay,' says Gran. 'If the house was dark or full of smoke, we wouldn't be able to find them easily. If they're in the door, we know where they are and can grab them on the way out.'

She sounds so calm, but I shudder at the thought of any emergency where we would have to find the keys in that much of a hurry. Or where we couldn't see through the smoke.

'Did you do this at your house?' I ask Jackson.

'Not this time. But we've done it at our last house when there were fires around.' He sounds very matter-of-fact about it. 'It happens every summer—there's a fire somewhere and people worry it will come close. But it never does.'

'Yet,' says Gran. 'But we shouldn't be too complacent.'

I know she's thinking of what happened in Canberra.

'Gran and Grandpa's house nearly caught fire in Canberra,' I explain to Jackson. 'Didn't it, Gran?'

Gran nods. 'Almost,' she explains. 'It got within a block or so of our house. Friends of ours lost everything.' She is quiet for a moment, and I bet she's remembering that day. She and Grandpa had to evacuate and didn't know till later that their house was okay.

Jackson frowns. 'That must have been scary. Mum asked Dad if we should stay home today,' Jackson says. 'But Dad reckons we'll be fine.' His frown disappears pretty quickly. Nothing ever seems to worry Jackson.

'Let's hope he's right.' Gran nods. 'But since we have nowhere else to be, we might as well practise being fire ready. Now let's do the outside,' she says, leading the way to the back door. We stop and put on hats and slather ourselves in the sunscreen Gran keeps on a shelf near the door.

It's hot outside, but there is work to be done. Gran gets a rake from the shed and has me rake up the leaves from around the yard. Jackson helps by piling them onto the compost heap. In the meantime, Gran has the hose out and sprays the whole garden.

'If things are damp, they're less likely to catch fire,'

she tells me.

This makes sense, but I can't see anything staying damp in this heat. Still, the water looks tempting. As if Gran knows what I'm thinking, she whips round and squirts Jackson and me.

We squeal and run away, but not very far. Getting wet makes us just a tiny bit cooler.

Gran's garden is struggling in the heat. Her little vegetable patch is wilting, even though she has only just watered it. Her tomato bushes droop sadly and her young lettuce plants look limp and very, very sad. The daisy bushes and geraniums in the garden along the back of the house look sad too.

The native plants look stronger. There are gum trees and bottlebrushes, and even a few ferns around the yard. I wonder which of these were planted by the previous owners and which ones just grew here from the surrounding bush.

Finished with the garden, I watch as Gran feeds the hose up onto the roof so that it rests in one of the gutters.

'What's that for?' I ask. It looks like she's planning on watering the roof.

'If a fire is coming, we'll turn it on and fill the gutters

before we leave. Helps to stop the house from catching fire,' Gran explains. She finds some rags and we use these to block the downpipes so that if we do fill them the water will stay in for a while. Gran seems so calm and organised. This reassures me. If Gran's not worried, I guess I shouldn't be either.

Finally, sweat pouring down our faces and inside our clothes, we head back into the house, collapsing on the couch in front of the air conditioner. Jackson and I guzzle ice cold water from the fridge as Gran reaches for her radio.

'It's so *hooooot*,' I moan, but Gran shushes us as a news bulletin comes on.

Soon Jackson and I are listening too as the announcer starts talking about the fires that have started around the state. I don't recognise the place names, but I see Gran frown several times. I wait until the list is finished before I ask.

'Are any of them close to here?'

Gran shakes her head. 'No, the closest is Kilmore, and that's not close enough to worry about at the moment. She heads across the room to her computer and opens up her browser. 'Still, I'd better keep an eye on the website.

Any closer to us and I think we should be heading into Melbourne.'

I can tell Gran is a little bit concerned, but I trust her. Jackson doesn't seem to be worried at all. Except when Gran suggests we don't go to the pool.

'Awwww,' Jackson and I say at the same time.

'But we're boiling!' Jackson adds.

'And you promised,' I beg.

Grans shakes her head. 'Sorry, guys. But things have changed. We need to be ready to leave, just in case. Hopefully this will all blow over and we can spend the whole day at the pool tomorrow!'

Jackson and I look at each other. I can see the disappointment on his face, and it mirrors mine, but we both know Gran is probably right. She has a fire plan, and it doesn't include heading down to the pool.

Jackson and I make some sandwiches for lunch, and then we all play a game of Scrabble, with Gran stopping every now and then to listen to the fire updates on the radio. The announcer lists the names of towns and districts that are being affected, and warnings to residents nearby. I'm glad that Marysville isn't mentioned, but amazed how many other places are.

'Some of these fires are really bad,' Gran says, shaking her head. 'This weather must make it nearly impossible to fight.' As well as the heat, there's a really strong wind blowing outside.

I'm busy trying to work out how best to use my 'Q' tile to try to catch up some points, but I hear the worry in Gran's voice. 'Are you sure we're safe here?' I ask.

'Sure as I can be,' Gran says. She doesn't sound quite as calm as before. 'The fires are miles and miles from here but if they get closer we can be in that car and on the road out in just a few minutes.'

'What about me?' asks Jackson, looking up from his Scrabble tiles.

'We'd take you with us, wouldn't we Gran?' I say quickly, imagining how bad it would be to be left behind in an emergency.

'Of course,' says Gran. 'We would head through Healesville anyway, so we would call ahead and let your folks know we were coming.' She stops and thinks for a moment. 'But it won't be necessary. We'll be fine!'

I wonder if she really means that. She has little worry lines above her eyebrows. I don't remember them being there before. But she smiles as she places her next word and counts up her points.

'Thirty-two,' she says, punching the air before writing her score down. 'Your turn, Jackson.'

I try not to think about the fire news as I concentrate on trying to beat Gran's score, which of course I don't do.

'You win, Gran,' I say finally. 'Do you wanna play again?'

Gran shakes her head, looking longingly at the book she has sitting next to her recliner. 'Why don't you two play something different while I have a little read?'

I take Jackson down to the spare room to choose a new game, but the photos hanging on the wall catch my eye. I look up the hall to where our bags are, and suddenly have an idea

'What are you doing?' asks Jackson as I carefully remove Gran and Grandpa's wedding photo and another one of them with Uncle John, Aunty Ev and Dad when they were little. And the one of Dad as a toddler playing with the hose. I slip the three photos into my packed bag. I don't answer, but Jackson seems to understand. He nods.

Just before I zip my bag back up, I spot my camera and have another idea. 'Let's take some photos,' I say.

Jackson quickly adopts a pose, with a big thumbs up and a goofy grin.

I giggle. 'Of the house,' I say, but I snap him anyway.

Jackson follows me around as I take some pictures. First the long passageway, which is one of my favourite parts of the house, with its polished floorboards and Gran's photo gallery.

Then the kitchen, with the dining table Gran says was the first piece of furniture she and Grandpa ever bought new. It's old, and has some scratches and dents, but I love it, and so does Gran.

Gran looks up from her book when we head into the lounge room and snap a few pictures, including one of her reading under the beautiful reading lamp Grandpa gave her for her birthday one year.

I think about the outside of the house, but decide it's too hot to go out there. Besides, I got a few snaps when Dad was cleaning out the gutters. Best wait till it's cooler to take any more.

I slip the camera back in my bag and soon Jackson and I are busy trying to beat each other at Snakes and Ladders. It's an old game, but still fun.

'Hah!' I say, some time later. 'I win again!' I punch

the air. 'At last I've found something I can beat you at.'

Jackson throws down the dice. 'Three times! I can't believe it!'

A snore from across the room makes us jump. Gran must have dozed off. We giggle, but quietly.

'What should we do now?' Jackson whispers.

'Dunno,' I say, glancing around the lounge room. 'Do you think the fires are out yet?'

Jackson shrugs. 'Why don't we check?' He gestures towards Gran's computer.

We cross the room to Gran's little desk and wiggle the mouse to wake the computer up. Gran gives another little snore. At least we haven't woken *her*. The internet is slow to load, and when I flick to the tab with the fire updates it seems to have stopped working.

'Internet is so slow up here in Marysville,' I whisper.

Jackson pulls a face. 'Yeah.'

I look at the radio next to Gran's chair, but she turned it off before she sat down, and if I turn it on now it might wake her.

We decide instead to read. I've brought my natural disasters book with me and I lend it to Jackson. He seems to like it almost as much as I do. Every time I look up from my own book—*Charlotte's Web*, which I found on Gran's bookshelf—I see him frowning in concentration.

I don't know how much time passes, but when I hear the sound of sirens coming from outside I jump.

'Was that a fire siren?' I ask Jackson.

'What?' he looks up from *Hard Times*. 'Sirens? Yeah, I guess it was.'

He seems to have been lost in the book just as I was in mine. We haven't even noticed that the light is dimming. I wonder how late it is.

I decide to wake Gran. As I head across to her chair, I reach to flick on the lamp, but nothing happens. Maybe the power is out. Now that I think about it, the air conditioner has stopped blowing out delicious cool air.

'Gran!' I say, giving her shoulder a gentle shake. 'Gran!'

Gran wakes with a start. 'Amy! What?' I watch as she comes fully awake, grinning sheepishly. 'Was I asleep?' she asks, looking at me and across at Jackson, who is standing on the other side of the chair.

'Yes,' I say. 'You must have been tired. But I think I heard a fire siren. And I think the power has gone out.'

Gran looks at her watch. 'Gosh—it's almost dinner

time,' she says. Then she realises what I just said. 'A fire siren? Are you sure?'

I nod. 'I think so. But not close.'

Gran looks at Jackson, who nods in agreement.

Gran gets up quickly and hurries outside, and Jackson and I follow. I realise instantly that there is a strong smell of smoke in the air, and Gran points to big grey clouds on the horizon.

'Smoke,' she says. 'That will be over in Kilmore.'

I'm not sure exactly which direction Kilmore is from here, but Jackson seems to know. He looks at me, and it's the first time I've seen him look a bit scared.

'Should we leave?' I ask. 'Just in case?' I don't care how far away the fire is—if we can see big grey clouds of smoke, it frightens me. My legs shake and there's a lump of worry in my throat. The smoke, too, is hurting my nose. It feels close. I strain my ears trying to hear the sound of sirens, but everything seems strangely quiet.

Gran takes a deep breath, frowning at the smoke. 'We might start getting ready,' she says. She must see the worry on my face because she gives me a little smile. 'Don't worry, Amy, Kilmore is really a long way away. We will just fill the gutters and wet down the gardens again, and then we might drive back to Melbourne.'

'What about me?' asks Jackson. 'Will you take me to Healesville?'

'Of course,' Gran says. 'I'll just text your mum.' She pulls her phone from her pocket. 'That's funny,' she says. 'Three missed calls. I didn't hear them.' Perhaps her phone was on silent, because Jackson and I didn't hear it ring either. 'One was your mum,' she says to Jackson. 'I'll just call her back.'

She presses the buttons, but purses her lips as she holds the phone to her ear. 'Nothing's happening,' she says. She stares at the screen. 'I don't seem to have any reception.'

'The internet wasn't working before either,' I tell her, remembering.

'I think we'd better get going,' says Gran. 'We might be able to pick up the emergency broadcast on the radio in the car, and find out what's what. And we can ring your mum on the road, Jackson.' Jackson looks at her gratefully. 'Now just help me lock up and get ready, will you?'

I try to stay calm, and get busy helping her go through her final checklist. Jackson helps too. While

Gran scurries around closing windows, locking up the shed and doing one last check of the house and yard, I turn on the hose she set up earlier to fill the gutters, and Jackson uses another one to wet down the garden beds around the house. But when I glance at all the smoke on the horizon, I can't help but wonder whether damp gardens will stop a fire big enough to make that much smoke.

Chapter 17

Listening in case we hear more sirens, we work quickly but calmly. Jackson and I don't say much. I'm worried but keep telling myself everything will be okay. If Gran isn't too scared and Jackson isn't too scared, then why should I be?

We get everything as wet as we can, and are turning off the taps when Gran calls, 'Okay, kids, let's go.'

She pulls her keys from the front door and backs her car out of the garage.

'You two get the bags and the blanket.'

'Why do we need a blanket?' I mutter to Jackson, not sure it makes sense.

'It's wool,' Jackson says. 'Fire resistant.' He picks up the blanket and Gran's bag.

Now it makes sense. I remember seeing a video about fire safety once at school. One thing suggested was to use a blanket to smother flames if someone's clothes caught fire.

I seriously hope we don't need to do that.

I pick up my own bag and the big bottle of water

next to it, and we head for the front door. As I look back down the passage, I hope it's not the last time I see Gran's house. It isn't exactly a mansion, but it is a lovely little cottage. I pat my bag, checking that I can feel my camera and those three photos. I'm glad that I thought to pack them.

As I come out of the house, something flutters down next to me. It's white and soft-looking, like snow. Then I notice other things fluttering around too. 'What—' Then I suddenly realise. Bits of ash. From the fires. Jackson must see them too. He stops, looking up at the sky, mouth slightly open.

'*Graaaan*,' I call as she climbs out of the car, dropping the bag and water bottle as fear rushes through me.

But Gran isn't looking at me. She seems to be looking over my head, her mouth open in shock.

When I turn, I see what she has seen. There is another mass of smoke, much closer than the other one, in the other direction. Huge grey-black clouds loom over the house. These ones are much, much closer than the ones we've been watching.

'Inside!' Gran calls, and I follow her, running through the door. My feet feel like lead. They don't seem to want to do what my mind is telling them to do. I feel Jackson's hand on my back, pushing me forward, and hear him puffing a little.

Gran runs to the back window and pulls back the curtain. We can see the smoke and, lower, an eerie rim of red on the top of the hill behind Gran's house. It seems to be getting dark very quickly too.

'Gran!' I say, panic flowing through my veins. 'Shouldn't we leave?'

Jackson agrees. 'Let's go!' he almost yells. 'Now!'

But Gran doesn't answer. She seems to freeze. She stands very still, staring at the scene outside, her mouth half open. Finally she swallows and speaks, in a voice I haven't heard her use before, quiet and old-sounding. 'I—don't—know,' she says. 'Maybe—my …' Then she looks at Jackson and me. 'The bathroom! We'll fill the bath with water. And …'

She hesitates again. I look out the window. In only seconds all the daylight has gone. It's black outside except for showers of orange sparks and flashes of red flame getting closer and closer. Then there is noise. So much noise. A roaring, and more distant bangs, like things are exploding. The fire is coming!

Gran is still frozen, looking out the window, her hand to her mouth. I think about her plan to shelter in the bathroom, then remember our promise to Dad to leave if things looked bad. This is bad. Very, very bad.

Jackson is looking at Gran, then at me, but he doesn't speak. No one is saying anything.

'No, Gran!' I say, surprised that my voice sounds so calm, when inside I am terrified. 'We have to go.'

She looks at me slowly, but doesn't react. I feel my blood rushing, but my mind is clear. 'We have to get out,' I say, barely registering that through the window behind Gran I can see her back fence burst into flames, and a shower of cinders falling onto her compost heap.

'Help me, Jackson!' I command. 'We have to get her to the car.'

I grab her arm and yank her hard. 'Now, Gran! Now!' She follows, stumbling a little, and I keep hold of her arm. There is smoke everywhere, and I don't want to lose her. 'Come on, Jackson! Gran!'

I lead the way, pulling Gran along the passage towards the front door. Suddenly Jackson is there, pushing Gran from behind. Our eyes meet as between us we push her out the front door. I grab the bag I dropped on the veranda and bring that with me.

I see Jackson do the same with the water and the blanket.

Outside, smoke stings my eyes and fills my lungs. I stumble towards the car, pushing Gran around to the driver's side. 'Get in!' I yell and, when she does, I slam the door, before running to the passenger side and throwing myself in. Jackson scrambles into the back seat.

'Let's go!' he says, his voice shaking. 'We have to go!'

Gran sits still, blinking in confusion, but I need her to drive the car. For a second I wonder if I could figure out how to get it going, but I realise that isn't going to work. I look round at Jackson, but he just stares back. He doesn't know what to do either. His face is pale and his eyes are wide with fear.

I remember something I saw in a movie once and wonder if it will work, but hardly have time to think. I lean across to Gran and give her cheek a slap. The sound shocks me and my hand tingles, but I don't have time to worry about that.

'Gran!' I say again. 'Snap out of it! And. Drive. This Car.' I say each word as a command, hoping against hope I will get through to her. Jackson is quiet, just staring at

Gran as if willing her to listen.

It works. Gran gives her head a sharp shake, blinking rapidly, and turns the keys, which are still in the ignition. The engine roars to life, not a moment too soon.

'Thank god!' I hear Jackson say. 'Please let's get out here!' He sounds really scared, and I don't blame him, but weirdly I feel calm now that we're moving. In some part of my brain I know that I need to stay focused to help Gran and Jackson. And myself, I guess.

An odd crackling noise comes from inside the car. I'm confused until I realise it's coming from the car radio. I jab at buttons, trying to make it stop.

As Gran puts the car into gear and steers towards her front gate I hear a *whoosh!* behind us and look back. Flames are shooting up the tree closest to Gran's house. A second glance and I see that her veranda has caught fire. Gran's house is on fire! A few seconds more and we would have been trapped in there. I don't tell Gran what I have seen. I need her to focus on getting us out of here.

In the back seat I hear Jackson gasp, and know that he has seen too. I glimpse behind, giving him a little shake of my head. I hope he understands what I'm trying to say *Don't tell Gran*.

Gran drives down the road, eerily dark except for the flashes of red and orange flames around us. At last she starts to speak, though she almost doesn't sound like my gran. 'No no no no *nooooo*,' she chants, echoing the word swirling around my own head. I'm not sure where we are going, where might be safe. The two roads out of Marysville go right through the bush, and if the bushfire isn't there yet, it soon might be. And Melbourne seems a long way away, and I don't know how long Gran will be able to drive for.

'Gran!' I say, remembering again something I saw on TV. 'We need to get somewhere open. Somewhere with no buildings or trees.'

My mind whirrs as I try to think where that might be. Marysville is full of trees, and completely surrounded by them. And it seems like most of them are on fire.

I turn to the back seat. Jackson is staring out of the window, his mouth hanging open and his hands gripping the car seat.

'Jackson!' I say, loudly. 'Where's a good place to go? Somewhere flat and open?'

Jacksons stares at me blankly for a moment, but then he says, only just loud enough for me to hear. 'The oval.'

In my mind I picture the oval near the park where Jackson and I played cricket. I remember there being trees and buildings around the edges. It was a big space, but hardly enormous. Still, there is nowhere else. Perhaps if we stay in the middle of the oval, we will be safe. Safe enough.

'Gran!' I say, tapping her gently on the shoulder. 'Take us to the oval!'

When she doesn't reply, I say it louder and more firmly. 'Gran! The oval! Now!'

Gran nods, her eyes on the road head. 'The oval,' she says, nodding slightly. 'We'll go to the oval. That's the place.' She sounds a little more like the sensible Gran I know, even though her hands are shaking violently and she is biting her bottom lip.

The trip through town is terrifying. We can hardly see through the windscreen, we are coughing and our eyes are streaming from the smoke, but somehow Gran manages to avoid hitting any of the dark shapes on the road that might be tree branches. Showers of flame and sparks surround us and there is a constant roaring in my ears.

I don't know if Jackson or Gran are saying anything.

It's too noisy, and I'm too busy staring at the road ahead of us. Ready to yell for Gran to stop if there's anything big on the road.

I see burning things on either side of the road. Trees, cars, houses. I hope there's no one in any of them. Some kind of animal runs in front of the car. It's too dark to be sure if it's a dog, a cat or some native animal.

It feels like we're on the road forever, inching down streets that are unrecognisable. I can only hope that Gran is aware enough of her surroundings to know where she is going. Once or twice she stops, looking from side to side as if not sure and, once, Jackson leans forward from the front seat and points out the road to our right.

I take my eyes off Gran and the road for just a moment to give him a grateful look. 'We'll be okay,' I say to him, hoping that's true.

He gives me an almost-smile then turns back to watch the road.

Finally we make it to the oval. 'This is it!' says Jackson.

Other cars! And lights! I can see the shapes of people moving about. Gran pulls up next to a truck and turns off the engine, but she doesn't move from her seat, just sits clutching the steering wheel and staring straight ahead.

'Gran!' I put my hand on her shoulder. 'Gran! It's okay. We're safe,' I say, again hoping that it'is true. There is still smoke and flame all around us, but being where there are other people makes me feel safer.

Gran turns and looks at me, as if only just registering that I'm with her. 'Oh, Amy!' she says, and bursts into tears. It makes me cry too. We hold each other and sob.

A noise behind us makes us both look round. 'Jackson!' says Gran weakly. 'You're with us!' She seems surprised, like she's just woken up.

Jackson is crying too. Gran reaches an arm towards him and he leans forward in the gap between the two seats. Gran and I hug him from either side and none of us says anything. We just shake and cry.

Chapter 18

A rap on the car window makes us all jump. A man stands outside the car. At least I think it's a man. He's holding some sort of cloth over his mouth, which makes it hard to see his face.

He gestures to Gran to open her window.

'Oh, it's you, Joan,' he says. 'Glad to see you're safe.'

Gran looks blank for a moment, but then seems to recognise the man. 'Hugh! We're here. Are we safe? I've got my granddaughter.' She points at me. 'And young Jackson.'

The man looks at us both.

'Are you all okay? No burns or anything?'

Gran blinks. 'I ...' She hesitates, looking at me.

I shake my head. 'No,' I say. 'But Gran's house—' I stop, remembering that Gran didn't see what I saw. The image of flames eating through her veranda and climbing the front wall is one that will stay with me forever.

Gran looks at me, understanding. 'Oh,' she says in a small voice.

The man's gaze goes between us. 'But you're safe,' he

says. 'As safe as can be, anyway.'

Across the oval I can see trees burning and hope they won't fall in towards it. And can the flames jump to the oval? I just don't know. It seems very small against the might of such a huge fire.

'Are my parents here?' Jackson asks, looking at the man. 'Have you seen them?'

The man shakes his head. 'I'm sorry, mate,' he says. 'I haven't.'

Jackson starts to cry again. I reach out and put a hand on his shoulder, not knowing what to say.

'They were in Healesville for the day,' Gran says. 'Hopefully they're still there.'

'Hopefully,' the man says sombrely.

'Come out of the car when you're ready. There's quite a few of us here.' He gestures towards the middle of the oval. I can see small groups of people standing or slumped on the ground. A few torches flicker, and some cars have their headlights on.

'Is that all?' asks Gran.

The man nods. 'There's maybe around a hundred or so here I reckon. The CFA volunteer told me some people left before the worst of it hit. I hope they got out okay. There were some police here.'

'And the firefighters? I know Gran is thinking about Dad.

'Some are still here, others have gone up to fight up at the mill at Narbethong. They're doing their best, but …' He pauses, his shoulders drop limply by his side. 'It's lost. Marysville's lost.' He walks slowly away, towards another car.

I can't believe what I'm hearing. How can the whole town be lost? But after what we've just seen, it makes horrible, terrible, sense.

Gran pulls herself out of the car, looking into the back seat. 'Have we got any water?' she asks me, and I realise some of what we'd gathered up got left behind. Gran's bag, and her papers, are still at the house. If there's any of the house left, which I very much doubt. But we do have water, thanks to Jackson. He holds out one of the two bottles and, as he climbs out of the car, he takes the blanket.

I climb out my side and walk around to where Gran is standing, looking bewildered. 'Water, Gran?' I say, taking the bottle from Jackson. She opens the lid and drinks a big gulp. Then she pours some into her hand

and splashes her eyes.

Suddenly I realise my own eyes are stinging too. I hadn't even noticed. I bet Jackson's are as well.

I take the bottle from Gran. 'Hold your hands out,' I say to Jackson.

He obeys me, cupping his hands, though he doesn't speak. I pour a little of the water into them. 'Now rinse your eyes,' I tell him. He does, blinking.

Then I pass him the bottle, and he does the same for me, before we each take a big gulp of water.

Gran is just standing looking around her. It seems like a ring of flame circles the oval, and, looking behind us, it is hard even to see the road we drove in on. And there are noises. Roaring flames, big crashes that might be buildings falling or buckling, and explosions.

A big bang makes me jump and squeal.

'It's okay,' says a man behind me. 'That'll be a gas bottle at one of the houses.'

I have to believe him. There's no way to know if he's right.

Jackson and I walk either side of Gran, guiding her closer to the group of people. Jackson spreads the blanket on the ground, and together we sit down. Some people are moving around; others, like us, seem frozen, not really knowing what to do. I wonder if help will come. There is a small fire truck parked nearby, but I know there is little one truck could do in a fire this size.

A man comes over to check on Gran. 'Are you hurt, Joan?' he asks. I realise it's the man that flirted with Gran that day. Jim, I think his name was.

Gran shakes her head, but doesn't say anything. Jim looks at her with concern.

'I don't think so,' I answer for Gran. 'But what should we do now?' I ask, since Gran doesn't.

'Wait, I guess,' Jim answers, shaking his head a little. 'And hope that someone comes.' He gives Gran an awkward hug before wandering off.

There isn't much else we can do, but it's a very long wait.

We huddle together, hardly speaking. I check Gran's phone, which has been in her pocket the whole time, but there is still no reception. I wish I could call Mum. Or Dad. Do they even know what's happening to us? I see that one of the missed calls is from Dad, and I listen to the message.

Mum? Mum, answer your phone. He sounds a

bit scared. *I need to know that you and Amy have left Marysville. It's not safe to be there, Mum. Get out now!*

The message was the last one Gran received. I wonder whether, if we'd heard it, we would be in Melbourne by now, safe.

I let Jackson listen to the message from his mum. *Joan, it's Gina. We're just leaving Healesville now. We've been watching the fire reports and we think we should come and get Jackson. Unless you could bring him to us. Ring me when you get this message.*

I look at Jackson, whose face is even paler than before. 'What if they *did* leave Healesville?' he asks. 'What if they got caught in the fire?'

'It'll be okay,' I say, trying to reassure him, even though I can't know if that is true. I don't even know if these fires stretch all the way to Healesville.

'I'm going to look for them,' he says. 'See if they're here.'

I'm a bit torn. I want to help him look for his parents, but I also want to keep an eye on Gran, whose face is pale and whose breathing is a bit funny. I half get up to follow Jackson, then sit back down.

I watch as he wanders to the nearest group, says

something, then, after a moment, moves to another group. I see people shaking their heads. When he comes back he's crying again, and I don't need to ask him to know that there is no news of his parents.

This time I don't try to reassure him. Instead, when he sits down I shuffle closer and put my arm around him, giving his shoulder a gentle squeeze just like Mum and Dad have done to me a million times when I've been scared or upset. On his other side, I see Gran shuffling closer too. She puts an arm around Jackson and gives me a tiny, sad smile. Maybe the Gran I know is coming back. I move a little so that I can touch Gran's other side, and we sit in a little close circle saying nothing, all lost in our own thoughts.

Over Gran's shoulder I watch the other people on the oval. Some are kids like us, and I wonder if any of them are Jackson's friends, Vin, Nathan and Tash. My friends too, I guess. Some people move about, others huddle in groups, or are even alone.

I can't see beyond the oval because of the smoke, but I remember looking at the hills behind while we were playing cricket. I also remember learning that fire goes slower downhill. Or was it faster? I wish I could remember. I hope that it's slower, and that it can't reach us here in the centre of the oval.

After a while I feel myself nodding off, and move to lie down. Gran and Jackson do the same. Unbelievably, the air has grown cool in spite of the smoke and fire, and we huddle close on the blanket. I drift into an uneasy sleep, waking too many times to count. I dream that we're stuck in the car, surrounded by flames, and wake, panting. Later I dream that I'm looking for Dad among burning trees. Not dreams, I guess. Nightmares. Each time I snuggle closer to Gran, listening to her breathing, which sounds rattly. At least if I can hear her breathing I know that she's with me.

Chapter 19

'Amy! Amy!' Jackson's voice wakes me.

I struggle to open my eyes. They're still stinging from the smoke in the air, and now something is dripping on me.

'What's happening?' I blink several times and see Jackson more clearly. It's starting to get light. Then I realise—the dripping is rain. I sit up, looking around me.

'Amy!' Jackson is squatting next to me. 'I think we need to cover your gran up. She's shivering.' I see that Jackson is shivering too. It's really cold. 'Could we wrap her in the blanket?' he asks.

While I try to work out how to do this, Gran wakes. 'Wha—' she starts, then stops. I see from her face that she has remembered where she is and what has happened.

'It's raining, Gran,' I say, stating the obvious, just to have something to say. Jackson and I help her to her feet and we put the blanket over our heads, hoping to keep some of the rain off.

Other people are stirring too. Or perhaps they haven't been asleep. 'We should move a bit,' Gran says.

Her voice sounds scratchy, but she is still more like her usual self than she was last night. 'It will keep us warm.' She starts to cough, and Jackson and I wait till she's finished before we start to move.

As the rain eases, we walk around the oval. Gran chats quietly with different people she knows. Many of them hug her, many of them cry and all of them seem unsure what to do next.

'All we can do is wait,' I hear a woman say. I wonder what we're waiting for. Help maybe. If anyone knows we even need help. It feels like the world outside of Marysville has ended.

We are cut off.

As it gets lighter, we can see beyond the oval towards the main street. Most of the buildings are gone, and the trees. Smouldering ruins line the road. Some people wander away from the oval, down the road, maybe to check on their houses, or maybe looking for a way out of town. I hope there is one.

A little dog yaps as it runs across the oval. I think it's the dog I took a photo of when I was in Marysville in January. I remember Gran saying that its owners, Jean and Harry, had lived here forever. That seems so long ago now. I wonder if they are okay.

I don't know how much time passes. Jackson and I lean against Gran's car, not saying much. Suddenly though, Jackson bangs the bonnet of the car with his open hand. 'They have to be alive! They just have to be!'

I'm shocked. Somehow I'd forgotten that poor Jackson must be super worried about his parents. Last night it was the last thing I thought about before I went to sleep. But this morning, concerned about Gran and surrounded by people in shock, injured or just plain worried, I hadn't thought to reassure him.

I jump up and give him a hug. I realise that it doesn't feel at all weird to be hugging a boy. At a time like this, hugs seem normal and necessary. Jackson hugs me back and cries. 'I'm so scared,' he whispers.

'I know,' I say, feeling bad that for a little while I had forgotten. 'But we'll find them.'

He doesn't see that I'm crossing my fingers, hoping against hope that they're okay. I wonder if it's okay to make a promise I'm not sure I can keep.

Gran comes over, walking very slowly and holding her phone. 'Still not working,' she says. 'I'm guessing the towers have all been damaged.' She notices Jackson's face.

'Oh, Jackson,' she says, seeming to understand what he is thinking. 'Oh, Jackson.' She doesn't tell him it'll be all right. I'm guessing she knows it might not be.

A distant sound makes me look up. It's something mechanical—a much nicer sound than the roaring and banging and crashing of the fire that we'd heard most of the night.

'A helicopter!' says Jackson, rubbing at his eyes.

'We're saved!' I say. 'Two helicopters.'

We watch as the helicopters land and, in spite of his worries, Jackson smiles at me. 'Help is coming!' he says.

Some people hurry towards the helicopter, but Gran tells us to stand back. After a while, though, she wanders over to the group talking to the new arrivals.

Jackson and I follow, watching to see what's happening. I see a camera and a microphone. 'Are they from the news?' Jackson asks.

I shrug. 'Must be. I was hoping they'd be rescuers.' My heart sinks a little, but then I see Gran holding something that makes me smile. 'A phone!' I say. It's bigger than Gran's mobile.

'A sat-phone!' says Jackson. 'Let's hope it works.'

The man who has passed Gran the phone helps her,

and after a few moments I see her smile and beckon to Jackson. He hurries towards her, and I watch as he speaks into the phone. Then he's smiling too, even as I see other people lining up to be next with the phone. I guess everyone wants to speak to their family.

Jackson hands the phone back to Gran and runs to me, smiling. 'They're alive!' he says, then bursts into tears.

This surprises me, until I see that he's still smiling. These are happy tears. 'They couldn't get through on the roads,' he says, explaining that they ended up staying in Healesville. 'They've been panicking all night but.' He hiccups a little sob, his smile fading. 'They th-thought I was dead.'

I find myself giving him another hug. 'But you're not,' I say. 'And they're not. You're all okay.'

Jackson pulls away and gives me a little smile. 'I'm not so sure about our house,' he says, looking down the street. 'But if I have Mum and Dad, that's the best thing.'

'Absolutely!' says Gran, who has come up behind Jackson. 'That's pretty much what your father just told me, Amy.' She smiles. 'He was beside himself all night, poor man. I think I'm in trouble with him for not getting out sooner.'

Now it's my turn to cry. Poor Dad. I wish I could hug him. And Mum. And Aaron.

Chapter 20

Dear Aaron

It was so good to hear your voice on the phone yesterday. I'm sorry if I scared you with all my crying. I seem to have done a lot of that the past few days. The doctor at the hospital said I was in shock, and that that was normal, but I couldn't help wondering if people like Captain Sully cried so much after their experiences.

It's strange to think though that all this time I've been fascinated with other people surviving natural disasters, I never once imagined that one day it would be me, trying to figure out a way to survive. We came so close to being caught in Gran's house when it caught fire. Another minute or two and I think we would have been trapped. And died, like lots of other people did. Gran says that I am her hero, because it was me who made her get in the car and drive away. It wasn't just me though—my friend Jackson helped. And Gran still did the driving. She is really sad about losing her lovely house, but she says she's lucky because she might have lost her stuff, but she's still alive and so am I. She cried a lot though when we picked her up from the hospital yesterday, and I don't blame her.

I think Dad cried too when he spoke to Gran on the phone

the morning after the fire. Gran said Dad was mostly relieved—but also a bit cross we hadn't left sooner. But who knows—if we left sooner, we might have been trapped on the road out. And then what would have happened?

So many tears. I don't know how much of the news you can see over there, but the stories of the fire are terrible. So many people have died and been injured. And Gran isn't the only one who lost her home. Most of Marysville is gone, and other towns too. The news keeps reporting it and interviewing people who've lost everything. A lady wanted to talk to me and Gran, but Dad sent them away. I'm glad. I don't think I want to be in the paper or on the TV. The only good thing about the reporters is that they lent people their phones when we were still stuck on the oval.

But there's good news too. People like Gran and me who survived. Families reunited with people they thought they'd lost. Like Jackson. When he and his parents were reunited, his dad whooped like he'd just won the lottery. And people just being so generous and helping each other. People from all over Australia are sending money and donating stuff to help out.

Speaking of good news, Dad just told me I have to finish off and send this—because it's time to go to the airport and pick up Mum. That's the best news of all. I can't wait to hug her.

Love you, my big brother.

Amy

PS. I know you meant it when you offered to come home. But even though I miss you heaps, I think you should stay there and keep having a wonderful time. Seriously, we're fine. Besides, I'm getting to eat ALL the ice cream. Dad is really spoiling me. Oh, and Buster is looking after me too. And besides, I'm hoping we can convince Gran to still go on her trip in May—and if you're still over there you can make sure she enjoys herself.
PPS. I'm attaching a photo of me, so you can see I'm safe—and also that I have definitely not been hiding anything from you.

In the car on the way to the airport, Dad is quiet. We don't listen to the radio, just travel in silence.

Finally, though, he reaches across and gives my shoulder a squeeze. When he speaks, I'm surprised that once again he sounds close to tears. 'You're amazing, Amy,' is all he says.

'Me?' I'm confused.

He shakes his head, smiling. 'Gran told me what you did.'

I blush, remembering that I slapped Gran. I hope I'm not in trouble. Gran hasn't mentioned it since the fire, and I'm hoping maybe she doesn't remember. 'What did I do?' I ask, finally.

'You saved her, Amy.' I watch him swallow. 'And yourself. You're a hero.'

Tears spring to my eyes. 'But I was scared, Dad. It was terrible.' I stop, not wanting to think about the walls of flame, the smoke, the awful sounds. The moments where I didn't know if we would make it to safety.

Dad squeezes my shoulder again. His eyes are still on the road ahead, but he shakes his head. 'You duffer! Of course you were scared! But you kept going. You used that fear to do what needed to be done. You got Gran into that car …' He pauses, and I wait for him to mention the slap, but he doesn't. 'You were like your heroes, Amy. You were brave. And because of that, I still have you. And my mum.'

This time he lets the tears trickle down his face and I realise I'm crying too. But inside I'm feeling warm. I remember what Dad said once about bravery.

'You said that before, Dad. About people finding the strength when they need it.'

He nods. 'And I was right, wasn't I? I told you you're braver than you realise.'

I smile, thinking of the heroes in the book Aaron had given me and wondering if they felt scared too.

'My book!' I say, thinking about it for the first time since the fire. 'My natural disasters book is at Gran's. It's—' I stop, realising that it has gone. The last time I saw it was when Jackson was reading it in the lounge room. Suddenly though, it doesn't matter. I shrug. 'Oh well,' I say. 'Maybe I'll have to find something new to obsess about.'

'Butterflies!' says Dad.

My mouth drops open. What is he talking about?

Dad grins. 'Or puppies. Or quiet beaches of the world.'

I wait for him to explain. I have no idea what he is getting at.

'Something safe!' he says finally. 'You've given me enough frights to last a lifetime.' His smile disappears. 'Seriously, Amy. That night was the worst in my life. When I couldn't get through to Gran on the phone, I thought …' His voice breaks and I watch him struggle to speak. 'I thought you were gone. I had no idea how to find you, or what I was going to tell your mum, or …' He stops speaking again and we're both quiet as he pulls into the carpark at the airport. When he finally parks though, he turns to me before we get out of the car. He pulls me into a hug. I hug him back, not knowing what to say. 'Now, let's go find your mum,' Dad says finally. 'I don't know what she's going to say about me letting you and Gran go to Marysville!' He pretends to shake. 'Not sure I'm brave enough to face her.'

We both laugh, wiping away the last of our tears. 'It's okay, Dad,' I say. 'I'll protect you!'

'Lead the way then, brave Amy,' says Dad.

I smile as I hurry towards the airport building. Dad might be right that Mum will have some questions, but mostly I just can't wait for her to give me a huge hug.

Chapter 21

'Amy!' Trudi is waiting for me when I get to school a week later. 'I'm so glad you're back!'

'Me too!' I say, and realise I mean it. I'm the happiest to be at school that I've ever been, and not just because I get to see Trudi. We've spoken on the phone a couple of times, but this is the first time I've seen her since the fire. Mum and Dad have kept me close by where they can see me, and we've all been looking after Gran as she recovers from smoke inhalation and shock and starts to deal with insurance claims and stuff.

So yes, it's wonderful to see Trudi. But as I look around the playground and across at the school buildings, I realise I'm very lucky to be here.

'It feels good to be alive!' I say.

Trudi giggles. 'Even if you have to go to school?' she asks.

'Even if I have to go to school!' I say, and mean it.

'Even if you have to sit next to Leith?' She gives me a sideways glance.

'Even if I have to—'

I stop, realising what she's just said. I look to see if she's joking, but she nods her head.

'Miss Evans changed our seating plan,' she explains, looking at me sympathetically.

I think about Leith, about how he has teased me in the past, and I realise something. 'Huh! Even if I have to sit next to Leith!' I say, and mean it, 'I'm not scared of him. I've seen and done much scarier things than that!'

'You're very brave.' Trudi smiles and puts her arm through mine as we walk towards our classroom.

'The good news is,' she says, 'that Leith might be next to you, but I'm across from you!'

'Huzzah!' I say, and feel a big smile spreading across my face.

Dear Jackson

I was so happy to get your email. I can't believe it's been a month since that horrible night. Sometimes it feels like it was just yesterday, and other times it feels like it didn't really happen to me, to us, at all. Do you feel like that? Mum's making me see the school counsellor to talk about it. She says it's important to understand what a scary thing we went through.

How about you? Do you think you'll ever forget what

happened?

How exciting that you have found a new place to live while your house is rebuilt. Is your new house nice? It seems too far away from here, but hopefully it won't be forever. And what about your new school? Poor you having to start at a new school. Will they rebuild the Marysville school, do you know?

Sorry about all the questions. I can't wait till you come and stay with us next holidays. You can meet my friend Trudi and we can go to the movies and play Scrabble. I was going to say we could play Scrabble with Gran, but I have exciting news.

Gran is going to Europe! She had booked the trip before the fire, but afterwards she wasn't sure. She said she didn't think she wanted to go any more. She was pretty down, and the smoke damaged her lungs. But today she came out of her bedroom smiling and told me she'd just confirmed her booking. She's leaving at the end of April, just as planned.

She says life is too short not to live it. She sounded just like she did back before the fire! I'm so happy.

I hope you are as happy as Gran. But don't go jetting off to Europe, will you? Maybe, when we're older, we can go together!

See you in a few weeks,

Amy

Chapter 22

'Go on, Amy,' says Mum. She smiles reassuringly.

Dad smiles too, gesturing to the front of the crowded room.

My legs shake like jelly as I head towards the man at the front of the room. The Premier of Victoria! He too smiles as he sees me coming forward and reaches out to shake my hand and slip a medal over my head. 'Well done, Amy,' he says.

The announcer, a woman with a microphone, waits till the people in the room have stopped clapping. 'Young Amy,' she says, 'receives this bravery medal for her actions during the terrible bushfires on 7 February this year. Amy was with her grandmother and another young friend in a house in Marysville. When they found the fire front bearing down on them, it was Amy's quick thinking on getting her grandmother, and her friend Jackson, into the car and away to the safety of the oval, that undoubtedly saved all three lives.'

The crowd claps again and I can feel my face growing hot. Everyone is looking at me. But I lift my head and look back. There are many people I don't know in the room, but some I do as well. Mum and Dad, of course, who have both taken the day off work, and my whole class. Miss Evan has organised a class excursion to the civic centre to see me get my medal.

I see Trudi smiling proudly and clapping so hard I wonder if her hands hurt. And our classmates clap too—even Leith, who I am surprised to see clapping nearly as hard as Trudi. He sees I'm looking, but he doesn't stop. Instead, he winks at me.

I look away, lifting the medal so I can see what is engraved on it.

For Heroic Deeds

There is one more person in the room that I know is clapping hard. My eyes come to rest on Gran, sitting next to her friend Jim, who I am surprised to see there. Gran is beaming, her eyes filled with pride. She sees that I'm looking and gives a thumbs up. I return the gesture. It's been two months, but Gran has never once mentioned the fact that I slapped her. I'm not even sure she remembers, to be honest. But as I look at Gran now, and down at my medal, I am kind of glad I did.

Dear Amy

Hello from Paris! Today Aaron and I went and saw the Mona Lisa. It really is a beautiful painting, but I mostly enjoyed seeing the crazy number of people who were crowding into the gallery to try and catch a glimpse or take a photo. Aaron and I lost each other for a little while, with so many other people crowding into the room.

I've also seen the Eiffel Tower, and tonight we are going to cruise down the river and see the tower all lit up. My tour guide says it is really most beautiful at night.

I'm so glad that you gave me the idea to take my first overseas trip. I'm seeing new things and meeting new people, and having such a lovely time. And after the last three months of sorting insurance and deciding whether to rebuild, and trying to replace all my belongings, being on holiday on the other side of the world is a nice break. It's helping me to forget about losing my lovely home, and that scary night we had.

But I do want you to know that I won't ever forget how brave you were that night. Without you I wouldn't be alive to be enjoying this wonderful holiday.

That's enough of the serious stuff. I have been busy learning how to get all the photos I'm taking on your camera onto my new laptop. When I figure it out, I'll send you some photos of all the things I've seen. And tomorrow I'll get a nice photo of Aaron for you too. And when I get home, what a lovely lot of photos I will have to add to the album you made me. How clever of you to rescue my three favourite photos from the house! Such a clever girl!

Say hello to your mum and dad from me, and keep smiling. I know I am.

Love,

Gran

HISTORICAL NOTES

Fire has played a significant role in the Australian landscape throughout its history, being used by Aboriginal people as a means of land management long before white settlement. In colonial times, however, the use of fire changed, with burning bush and grasslands seen as dangerous and hard to control.

Since white settlement, the threat of bushfire to land, property and people has been an ever-present threat, especially in summer, and there have been many large-scale, tragic fire events. But no fire has been as devastating as the Black Saturday bushfires of February 2009.

Already suffering the effects of a long drought (known as the Millennium Drought), Victoria was in the midst of another very dry summer. At the end of January, the daily maximum temperature was over 43 degrees for three consecutive days, with a peak of 45.1 degrees on 30 January. With the Victorian bush being very dry from the drought, and humidity levels low, authorities knew that the bushfire risk was high. On 6 February, Victoria's Premier John Brumby warned that the following day was forecast to be the worst for fire conditions that the state had ever experienced.

Fires were already burning in some parts of the state, including in the Bunyip National Park, but on 7 February, the Premier's prediction proved well founded. Temperatures across the state rose quickly to 40 degrees, later peaking at 46 degrees, and strong winds (over 100 kilometres per hour) added to the problem. The first fire of the day started when the wind blew power lines down in the Kinglake area. Storm-force winds fanned the flames and soon other fires broke out in other areas, some started by arsonists. The strong winds meant that embers spread quickly, and soon there were over 400 individual fires, many of which merged to join huge fire fronts. Firefighters worked hard to do what they could, but the scope of the fires was unfathomable, fires spreading rapidly and often in thickly forested areas. Thousands of Country Fire Authority firefighters and many other government and private agencies did all they could, and in many cases saved lives and buildings. In spite of this, the fires took several weeks to fully control, such was their scope.

In all, 173 people were killed in or as a result of the fires, with 414 injured. The number affected by the psychological impact is not known. Over a million animals (native and domestic) are believed to have died, and 450,000 hectares of land was burned. Houses, schools, businesses, farm buildings and more were lost, including in the town of Marysville, where this story is set. The fire that hit Marysville started at Murrindindi at around 3 pm, and hit the town of Narbethong before finally reaching Marysville at 6.45 pm, destroying all but fourteen buildings in the town. Many of the townspeople left the town shortly before the fire hit, when police led a convoy of people who had sheltered at the oval. Others, though, did not receive warnings or did not have time, and about seventy people sheltered on the town oval during and immediately after the fire. Forty-five people died in this fire.

The Victorian Premier John Brumby described Marysville after Black Saturday, saying 'There's no activity, there's no people, there's no buildings, there's no birds, there's no animals, everything's just gone.'

Other major fires on Black Saturday included fires at Beechworth, Bendigo, Bunyip State Park, Central Gippsland, Coleraine, Dandenong Ranges, Horsham, the Maroondah/Yarra region, Redesdale, Weerite and Wilson's Promontory.

The aftermath of the Black Saturday fires was huge. The cost to human life, the death of animals, the destruction of forests and the impact on houses, buildings and infrastructure were immense.

A Royal Commission estimated the cost of the fire to be $4 billion.The short and long-term impact on the people affected is impossible to measure and, ten years on, the effects are still being felt.

Ten Things YOU Can Do to Fight Global Warming

1. Walk or ride your bike whenever you can
2. Car pool or catch a bus
3. Turn off the lights – only use electricity when you have to
4. Unplug appliances when not in use
5. Recycle – paper, plastic, metal
6. Avoid unnecessary plastic
7. Drink tap water instead of buying it in plastic bottles
8. Don't waste food
9. Grow your own fruit and vegetables
10. Make your garden water-wise with mulch and native plants